Food Porn

Sienna Liu

Food Porn

Copyright © 2024 by Sienna Liu

ISBN: 979-8-9899400-3-5

Cover design by Catherine Weiss.

Edited by Story Boyle.

www.gameoverbooks.com

For Frankie,
my only anchor in reality.

"But thou has suckled me with a bitter milk: my moon and my sun thou hast quenched for ever. And thou has left me alone for ever in the dark ways of my bitterness: and with a kiss of ashes hast thou kissed my mouth."

—James Joyce, *Ulysses* (1922)

"We're not sluts. But when we are, it's for an egg."

—Instagram, @eatingfortheinsta (2017)

Black coffee is good. Even better if you also have a banana, because if you eat your banana with your coffee your banana tastes like ice-cream. It felt indecent, somehow, to be devouring a banana during my nine o' clock seminar while the professor was talking about disconnection and différance and de-differentiation and Deleuze and Derrida, among other d-words. So yes, I was studying comparative literature and I was mildly illiterate. By that I mean, I was only amenable to things that sat well with other things that had long solidified in my heart, or my mind, whichever is more impenetrable. I was deconstructing my banana, when the professor went on to talk about those two fundamental truths of the human condition. First, the most important thing about life is that we are going to die, our existence is a death sentence, and god is the first murderer because he makes us mortal. Second, the truly existentially horrible thing is the present. Nothing we are doing is really justified. Our daily routine is merely avoidance behavior. I chewed my banana and wondered whether any of my gestures were truly authentic by that logic, such as how I was handling the situation with this coffee and this banana. At the same time I was also thinking about whether any of this could feed into my thesis on food porn. Then I got distracted by the hand of the guy sitting in front of me, who was doodling scenes of obscenity on his notepad. He was German, and because of that he spoke English with the usual cruelty of non-native speakers.

For instance, he once said, referring to our professor who just entered the room, wow it's like Death himself just walked in.

After class I stretched myself all out on the lawn in front of our departmental building. Frankie's class ended at the same time but in a building far, far away. It would take her a while to catch me. I lit a cigarette and smoked with my back against the cold grass. A second later the German guy walked by, noticed me, and started to talk about some book. I sat up and he talked while standing. I nodded from time to time. Then he said it was outrageous that our readings were all excerpts. One should definitely expect students at the graduate level to read at least two complete books a week, no? Indeed I said, though I don't know if it's possible to read *Life and Fate* in a week, I get your point. He took an interest in me because I was the only undergraduate in that seminar and he found every opportunity to impart a lesson. Finally he left, apparently quite satisfied with himself. I lay down again and checked my messages. There were a few from you.

You were talking about grains and vegetables being
the great inventions of men
that men and vegetables condition each other, that rice
is what rice is today because we have been cultivating it
for thousands of years
that evolution is an illusion
a hope conjured up by our linear perception of time
or should you say, one hope
or should you say, perception of linear time.
I had my eyes closed for a second. I could smell freshly cut grass, bacon and butter biscuits from the cafeteria, and a mixture of colognes sending various signals
and I replied to you:

(I'm lying on the ground, by the way,)

if we are necessarily limited by our perception

or should I say, unmediated perception.

And you replied:

if you are lying on a ground as big as yourself.

We were both confused by what the other said, perhaps. And for some reason that confusion prompted you to talk about Kafka

or should I say, Kafka's books.

You said your landlord had a few Kafka that he left all his Calvino Borges Bulgakov Dostoyevsky Kafka behind and

went to law school

that he sublet his apartment and moved into a place down the street

with his girlfriend

and he was a happy person free from some torture.

I saw Frankie walking towards me, upside-down with her black sunglasses and black ripped jeans and black leather bag. As Frankie became more concentrated in my vision I was struck by how much we dressed alike, or should I say, how much I dressed like her. She sat down next to me and asked for a cigarette. The sun was just out, pouring and pouring on the thin snow gathered on grass. For a cigarette's time we were both busy texting someone else. The guy Frankie was texting was a philosophy student who loved free association and rhyming. Frankie was trying to come up with words that rhyme with *drool*. She replied, Istanbul. The philosophy guy said, failed. Frankie said no, depending on how you say it. The guy said ugh. Frankie said haha but I will say this is more fun than I thought. Then the guy said fish is door gun fan guy bought. Then he said yeah that's true I don't want it anymore

I don't think I need it anymore I don't know why I didn't feel like it anymore I don't. Yeah that's what happened when we did this snow day at work today and we all had fun together we got the same stuff together together and together together. Frankie shoved this message in my face as if she thought I out of all the people in the world should understand. I read it and told her very sincerely I wasn't sure either what he was getting at. Frankie took off her sunglasses, sighed, and declared that she was fed up with these intellectual, ethereal men.

We went to a coffee shop on Broad Street and sat at a table next to the window. Outside our window were cherry trees that were not blossoming, not yet, but soon. Next to our table were plants in smaller pots which, in retrospect, now that I know more about indoor plants, might have been coffee plants. Frankie got a goji-cacao superfood oatmeal and a black coffee. I got a popsicle. Cookies and cream. I stuck that popsicle into my mouth and stared at my screen, at the first few lines of my thesis. Various people had warned me that I should never start with the opening, but I wouldn't know what to do with the rest of it if I didn't get the opening right. I had written:

> What is sexy about food porn? Dislodged from the kitchen, food, devoid of its nutritive or taste qualities, enters the realm of the performative.[1] We all have that experience, catching ourselves mesmerized by an Instagram post of the very moment when the dripping syrup lovingly pours over the steaming pancakes.

1   By "performative," I am emphasizing the dominance of a food item's visuality or appearance, as opposed to its nutritional functions. I'm also using the word to describe various ways in which food porn is an ongoing and socially constructed domain (via practices such as image sharing, tagging, commenting, etc.), in a similar vein to Judith Butler's description of gender as performative, and how some language is performative à la John L. Austin.

We find it—the carefully framed picture—flirtatious. It seduces. It makes us really, really want a pancake with real, shimmering maple syrup. Captivated, we gaze at these photos of exposed food as they tease us with their sensuality. This desire to look rarely has anything to do with real hunger; instead it says something about the voyeuristic pleasure in our interactions with the visual capacities of food, a pleasure evocatively named "#foodporn" according to social media conventions. By engaging visceral, and "fleshy" elements, the performative aspect of food imagery invites ostensible comparisons with sex,[2] such as this Instagram post of a gooey egg sandwich [NTD: insert picture of gooey egg sandwich]. This thesis concerns itself with everything you will ever want to know about food porn but are afraid to ask.

Re-reading this I could feel my stomach throbbing so I had to take a sip of Frankie's black coffee. Frankie never said a thing about my eating habits. She stocked her fridge with ice-cream and juices and could go without a real meal for days. In those days we pictured eating as something spontaneous and even a bit reckless. There was nothing ritualistic about the way we did it—the way we ate—and we would like to keep it that way so that we would `never become one of those people who ate the exact same thing at the exact same hour every day, which seemed to be the surest step to a mid-life crisis at which point you suddenly realize you have been ruled by, what is it called, a regiment? A regimen.

We sat in that coffee shop until it closed. From time to time I texted you again. I remember at one point you told me you were taking a shower, because the heater had been sending

2 Andrew Chan, "'La Grande Bouffe': Cooking Shows as Pornography," Gastronomica 3, no. 4 (Fall 2003): 47–53.

you sweats and you were too lazy to adjust the temp. I replied that it was quite impressive, the level of your laziness. And you said actually in your opinion it was your way of phrasing it that was more impressive. And I said well this hubris is not good for your soul. Then I thought about whether I should say something about me being too lazy to eat, that all I ate that day was banana and ice-cream, but I decided against it. When the shop was about to close and I was looking out wistfully and seeing nothing at all worth writing about, Frankie suggested we go to a real restaurant for dinner. Research for your thesis, she said. Then I'll have to apply for more funding, I said. We ended up going to Piedmont, her favorite. For the longest time we thought the name was French or Italian, until this day when we were eating dessert and, bored from the eating, we googled it and found out that Piedmont is actually a plateau region that crosses several southern states, or at least that was how the restaurant got its name. When we were digging into the lava cake Frankie and I discussed how little we knew about this country in which we had been living for four years, and how much longer we would still be living here. It was depressing.

I'm getting fat Frankie said, as she made a gesture signaling that she was unbuttoning her ripped jeans under her sweatshirt. Me too I said, but it's okay, it's still winter. It suddenly occurred to Frankie to take out her phone and get a picture of the half-eaten lava cake. As she was doing that, I looked at the cake for a few seconds, zooming in on the dark liquid dripping, melting, flowing, and thought about its material connection to sensuality. It is conventional in Instagram food posts to use the present continuous tense, but the *-ing* is not a truthful account, at least not the whole picture, of what happens (is happening) here, for the present continuous tense prescribes motion, a piece of time, a lived experience. What we see here, instead, is a frozen image, which is always at once an embodiment and a denial of the passage of time. What further complicates the situation is that this frozen image, fixed, unchanged, unchangeable, is also made perpetual in its circulation. Capturing a moment in motion lets us imagine a temporality that flows beyond the specific image, beyond the present. It lets us imagine a pleasure that is not restricted to particular, temporarily discrete acts, but a long history of pleasure, a flowing continuity, and a moving world out there beyond the frame of representation. I was feeling nauseous, from the wine, the cake, or the words and phrases that were giving birth to themselves in my head, in particular *constellations of desire.*

Which filter do you prefer, Frankie asked as she handed her phone to me. I said, Amaro. I always preferred Amaro because the name originated from a liqueur. All dizzy and unspeakable. The filter lived up to its name. The lava cake was looking like it was inviting us to get up close and personal.

We returned, slumped and heavy, to Frankie's apartment. An apartment with gigantic exposed pipes and walls of the most vibrant red. I was sitting on her floor, playing the guitar, playing with the guitar, actually. Meanwhile Frankie was looking for something in her walk-in closet. It was so big that it should really be called a sleep-in closet. From time to time, Frankie shouted things at me through the red wall, this or that guy, mostly. After a while Frankie finally emerged from her closet with an off-the-shoulder black top and a pair of really short shorts in faded blue. She was putting on earrings in front of the mirror. When Frankie walked—and she loved walking around without a definitive purpose in her enormous apartment—you would think she was dancing. There was something musical in how she moved that I just had to stare at her legs. I couldn't help it. Looking at herself in the mirror, Frankie said to me, to fuck without love, you know, is a glorious thing that you should try sometimes. I smiled at her in the mirror. Frankie knew, and felt very attacked by the fact that at this point of my life I had only really slept with one person. Until very recently, I was still madly in love with an intellectual, ethereal guy who dumped me for beautiful boys, or, should I say, the potentiality of beautiful boys. I said to Frankie, sometimes I really wish I had a penis. I think what I have is this more literal version of penis envy, not the kind we read in literary criticism or theory, no. I look around and see walking penises and really, really want to chop them off and lock them up in display cases made of beautiful glass. They do have a point when they talk about the castrative power in some women. Frankie gave me a look that weighed like misplaced compassion.

Frankie was determined to go out. Tuesday nights are for Franklin Street. She asked if I wanted to join and told me who else would be there. I briefly imagined the type of conversations we'd have and declined. She took another two minutes to adjust her hair, and then she swung the door shut. I lay down on her floor again. With Frankie out of the picture I abandoned myself to the turmoil in my stomach.

> I had been texting you non-stop, by the way
> and at this point I told you I felt the need to
> empty myself. Then I did.
> I threw up everything into Frankie's pristine porcelain
> > toilet and felt
> lighter in a strange ecstatic way. You asked

what happened. I returned to the floor with
a hollowness that was
all-encompassing and told you
I don't know. Might be food poisoning
and when I typed that I realized I didn't like saying
anything concrete to you like that
because I never wanted you to speculate about the inner
workings of my body and
to my great relief you said something like
maybe one of those food ingredients didn't like to work
with the rest.

I sat near the edge of Frankie's balcony, lit a cigarette, and looked down. The swimming pool down below looked like a giant sanitary pad. For some reason I wanted to jump right in from her balcony on the fifth floor. I really wanted to jump. The temptation was enormous. I had to keep asking myself in my mind to please please please don't jump. Then I got hungry again and circled around to reach Frankie's fridge, careful not to drop any ashes from my burning cigarette, and took out a tub of ice-cream.

I went back to smoking and ice-cream eating and texting at the same time. It was incredible how many hands and mouths I had at my disposal. You sent me a number of things.

You told me you had been revitalizing your fantasy and fascination
for mundane desires
so a goal, a common goal, is good
like the pursuit of a great voice, or, people's breaths,
you said,

and their scents, you look into their eyes and they'll do
crazy things in response
(oh the texture of their voice I said.)
yes you said
but you said you had yet to encounter a great voice,
outside cinema, at least
(the vibrations and variances I said.)
yes you said, and the accents and rhythms
diction
(and I said, I have yet to encounter anything great
outside cinema (well not really))
and you said, greed is good
desire is good
appetite is good
down with the monotheists
want is good.
(And when you said that I was thinking, and you are
good, you are very very good. And I asked you, do you really
believe all that?)
nope, you told me you couldn't really be fluent
now that you came to think of it
you don't write about desires
(and I thought, my desire is something about which I
cannot be fluent, now that's a good line.)
Then you made a prophecy. You prophesied that I
would eventually
tell you everything, everything, all the secrets I kept like
things I wanted to say but didn't
and you said
about to sleep, or fall asleep

whichever comes first.

I didn't reply after that. It was nearly four and you should sleep. You drank too much and slept too little. I smoked too much and ate too little. I thought about this void and this excess and I smoked one cigarette after another until I was not really feeling anything disturbing. What are the things I really wanted to say but didn't? Too many. All my/our sadness, frustration, envy, and self-doubt seemed to stem from this inability to speak. Perhaps it is true. Perhaps it is indeed the case that we, women, have something else, some shortcut, forever beyond the symbolic order, which, after all, is an order built upon the name of the father. We are said to have something else, but because that something else is beyond the reach of language we could never say anything about it. So we fall into our predetermined silences. All the theoretical terminologies were flooding in my head and I welcomed the tides, the warm embrace of those letters and words and phrases that refused to be spoken, and at that moment my only wish was that I could figure out what it was, what it was I really wanted to say to you.

At a certain point that night I realized I was still awake. The acidity of time in my mouth tasted like an afterthought. I sat up on the floor. Then I understood I had not always been awake, in fact, something woke me up. A voice. A hail. My name. Yes yes someone was calling my name. Waking like that from a cold floor with your own name resounding in your entire being, your entire consciousness, was like being called into existence. The whole world rushed in violently in those first few seconds, and I couldn't quite figure out what my place was in that world. Not yet. I looked outside the window and I could trace two vague figures on one of the other balconies, where I thought the sound of my name was coming from. I thought I saw Frankie, and someone a lot taller than Frankie. The two figures were smoking. I saw little red flames flickering as one of them took a drag. This could all be a dream, later on I would think, but at the time on that floor I thought I distinctly heard Frankie calling my name, again and again, from the balcony that was facing mine, or hers. I saw her wave at me. I waved back. I wasn't sure if she saw it.

She saw it. Of course she did. She said so when I climbed into her car the next morning at the bus stop. A few minutes before that, when I was waiting for Frankie to pick me up, some people were giving away donuts next to the bus stop. They had a huge sign raised over their heads: Donuts for Diversity, with two capital D's. I gladly took one. Donut, not Diversity. Diversity is, lamentably, not countable. I was chewing my donut, concentrating on that defining hole in the middle, the hole that makes the donut whole, while thinking about what this hole could mean. This core emptiness around which desire runs and runs until it exhausts itself. In that sense Diversity and Desire are both lost causes.

For some reason Frankie called the guy Donut. I climbed into her car still chewing a real donut, so I didn't immediately respond when she asked, hey, what do you think of Donut? I was still chewing the last bit, or bite, of my donut and I said, so I wasn't dreaming. No of course you weren't she said, you waved back! And this guy on the balcony, I asked, isn't the same guy who studies philosophy and free association? No no, not him, Donut is new, he actually lives right next door and he's the complete opposite of the philosophy guy. With Donut it's easy and fun. The deepest conversation I can have with Donut is, for instance, whether ripped jeans are problematic because they are fetishizing poverty. Oh, I said, that is nice. Fun is nice I said. Donut, tall and lean. Donut spelling out social commentary. I couldn't really square these two images with one another, probably because the image of a donut is inevitably round. I think I might have even told Frankie that, that he didn't strike me as a Donut. Frankie just shrugged and said she thought the nickname could be an antidote to his flamboyant masculinity. Right I said. We looked ahead. Some song with a lot of guitar chords was playing at full blast in Frankie's car. She opened the sunroof and the scent of lingering winter—smoky, sweet—rushed in. I was feeling light in the head again. I turned to look at Frankie. She was wearing her sunglasses so I couldn't tell whether she was feeling lightheaded too, whether easy and fun was doing her any good. Frankie sipped her iced latte. My donut was gone.

Do you want to get something to eat, I asked. Actually no Frankie said, I ate too much last night so I'm going to starve today if that's ok. Can we go for coffee? Right, yeah of course, I said. Two things everyone knew about Frankie were that Frankie cared about what she ate and Frankie drove very well. She had been driving everywhere since she was sixteen while I was still walking and walking in a city with many narrow streets and opportunities for digressions until blisters started growing between my toes. I still wore socks back then. Some years after that I quit. I quit wearing socks and I quit wearing bras, though both are meant to protect us from experience and age. I was still reflecting on the thickness of my soles when Frankie began to talk about her thesis. Her thesis also had to do with the body, with the tiny things that got trapped in our lungs and how external forces, such as neoliberalism, exacerbated those internal processes of destruction. Frankie was asking me whether a certain way of looking at Chinese society makes sense to me, whether Badiou has any value here (or there, since we were driving around in a nondescript little town in the southern United States). I nodded. I said yes, yes of course. But I wasn't entirely sure.

We stopped by Orange Street. It took Frankie a while to find a parking spot and she took the chance to flesh out her arguments. My understanding of that part of her thesis was forever juxtaposed with the image of that gloomy, silent parking lot where things squatted darkly at the corner. So basically, she concluded, we are fucked by neoliberal individualism within the domain of the family. Okay, I said. She was walking through the door of the coffee shop ahead of me. Always a few steps ahead of me. I watched the dry ends of her hair and the dead ends of our sentences.

The coffee shop served all their drinks in bowls. I got a ginger latte and Frankie got a lavender one. Mine tasted like medicine and hers tasted like incense. We sat outside and undressed our laptops. I sipped my latte, sighed, and began to type:

[Notes - Chapter on History]

The term "food porn" was coined in 1979 by Michael Jacobson to "connote a food that was so sensationally out of bounds of what a food should be that it deserved to be considered pornographic."[3]

"What a food should be" introduced a distinction between legitimate and illegitimate desires.

"Sensationally out of bounds" means the deliberate eroticization of food imagery.

Initially a derogatory term; now, increasingly neutralized, and valorized even, with the rise of social media. We are in an age where everyone, it seems, is engaged in the

---

3   Anne E. McBride. "Food porn," *Gastronomica: The Journal of Food and Culture* 10, no. 1 (Winter 2010), 38.

act of styling and capturing food on mobile devices; everyone is either receiving or extending an invitation to gaze, vicariously consume, and produce.

According to Webstagram, which ranks Instagram images by popularity, food images retain popular resonance through various hashtags such as "foodporn," "yummy," "yumgasm," and "dessert." Amongst all the competing tags, "#food" figured as number 25 in the top 100 tags on Instagram in 2014.[4] As of February 19, 2017, the hashtag "#foodporn" has been attached to 115,811,310 posts.

The coffee shop was famous for its pies, or so they thought, because their website was www.fantasypie.com. Brown Butter Pecan, Pear and Walnut, Lemon Chess, Vanilla Sugar. People around us were all busy styling their pies, pushing the crumbs together or arranging the pear slices on top. With one leg folded on their chair, they had their phones hovering above their pies like they were scanning them. Camera eats first, no doubt. I almost wanted to ask them: hey, so, I'm just curious, why do you take pictures of your food? Will you look at those pictures again? Will you post them on social media? Why would you get several takes from the same angle? Do you, perhaps, believe each take is slightly different? But I didn't ask anything, in the end. If I were to do that—to really get out there and interview people—I would lose control of the things I wanted to say. Other people's voices would defy me. And I would be dishonest if I pretended I never heard them. Now, with a lavender latte mustache, Frankie, for some reason, was speaking longingly of a very good apple strudel she once had in Vienna. A very cold day when museums were not yet open and she was walking aimlessly in the city

4   Yasmin Ibrahim, "Food Porn and the Invitation to Gaze: Ephemeral Consumption and the Digital Spectacle," 3.

until she stopped at a café that looked proud, proud of being old. In fact the café looked as determined as this trip of hers. Frankie knew no one in the city, and she didn't tell anyone she was going. And this detail—her wandering in the city unknown, unknowing—seemed to be very important. She was studying abroad in Europe, a continent she would always remember to be very cold (not literally) and very expensive (literally). She wasn't very happy in Europe, I deduced, since she talked so little about it. Actually, all I could gather from what she told me were a series of hasty impressions. Of classes that were both demanding and meaningless. Of frivolous friendships. Of bunk beds and solitary trips. Even though she mentioned the episode with the apple strudel almost like a footnote, to me it was the only tangible thing about that particular version of Frankie, during a year when I was still trapped in this small town dreaming about other places. So, it was November and the city acted like a blond little boy who didn't want to get out of bed. All day long Frankie had been walking along the tramlines, admiring the streets and squares and speculating about their history, listening to some album that she carefully chose so that it would come to define this city in her recollection. It was November but it was already very cold—she had to reiterate this point. So cold that she was shuddering in the wind. In her thin brown jacket. In front of this very old café. With its ridiculously high ceilings and tinted windows. She walked in. She sat down by the window. She picked the first item on the menu, not so much a fateful decision that was often overstated in films, but one out of an absent-mindedness, of letting life happen to you just like that and not engaging with it with any deeper commitment. She looked up after she pronounced the name to the waitress, and she remembered that the waitress had startling green eyes and a grumpy face. The apple strudel came, messy and probably authentic. She ate it with whipped cream. She didn't like cream, usually. Whenever we got pancakes at a diner she would specifically ask to please not give her any cream. But that day in Vienna when the cream came with the strudel she ate it, because it came that way and it seemed non-negotiable—that pretty much summed up her experience in that foreign continent: the loss of all bargaining power. Sahne, she said. Which doesn't really sound like cream, does it? It sounds a bit harsh, while cream is supposed to be all lightness and air. But she had to accept that as well.

Yeah no it doesn't, I agreed. I picked up my bowl of ginger latte again and drank the way I imagined heroes in old mythical tales would drink their rice wine before heading up a mountain to fight a tiger. I had no tigers to fight. I had no mountain to climb. I put down the bowl and picked up my phone. Frankie asked me who I was texting. I said, without looking at her, oh the guy who's making films. Frankie gave out a tiny noise of disapproval. She must be thinking that I was, again, trying to make things difficult for myself. She glanced at whatever I was composing on my phone and shook her head slowly. Who is this person, anyway, Frankie said, do you know anything about them? Yeah, I said. I told Frankie that you were from the same city, you were a few years older and you were making films in New York. Also, you drank a lot. Also, you claimed to have been studying hypocrisy but dropped out at some point because you drank a lot. You knew all the books I was reading. You told me things.Inconsequential things, trivial, even, but I liked the way you talked about them. As I continued to paint a portrait of you I realized Frankie was stirring her latte like it was a milkshake.

So, Frankie asked, will you try to go see him? I don't know I said, is that important? She giggled—she was distracted by her own text messages. After a few minutes Frankie turned to me again, and explained to me that I had this tendency of romanticizing people in the abstract and it would be best for me to see you as soon as possible so I could be disappointed before it's too late. What is too late, I asked. She didn't respond to that. Instead she sipped her latte and said, you are only obsessed with him because you are homesick, and really, I don't know what's the attraction of men from Shanghai. Frankie had a point, I had to admit.

Then she started to write. When Frankie began to write the air seemed to be going her way. Everything pointed to her. The sun. The air. My thoughts. I felt out of breath. I looked at my phone—while we were discussing you, you were still sending lots and lots of messages. I stared at the words you sent over. I read them again and again, while new words continued to appear, calling upon each other, canceling out each other, giving rise to new meanings and new confusions.

In your narration you were always cold and bored
drunk or sober
which was the same thing
and (still) hungry.
You would mention the food items in your vicinity and describe to me how you would devour them without relish.

An existence drenched in the syrup of sadness, sealed with silence.

On this particular day I saw you as a snowing person in the dark.

I didn't know why I would have this image of you literally snowing, soundlessly, snowflakes dropping from your hair and lashes and vanishing into the long grass and you would

give out terrible smiles when you were smiled upon.

Perhaps I had seen that image in a dream because sometimes

I woke up believing I had seen, in my dream, someone who pretended to be you and I was angry,

that this someone would play such a prank on me.

It was my way of grappling with the significance of it all, I guess, of the minutest details of a life that was still, perhaps always, unknown to me, the strangest, most incoherent thoughts a person could have, and you were sharing them second by second.

I wondered if sending me all these things was your way of giving yourself to me in pieces, though I wasn't sure what to do with them. I was sure of one thing, though, that the words were real, that they were breathing creatures with such uncanny, unapologetic faces that they might alarm others who are not familiar with the face of the truth. I was so sure of their truth that once in a while I would say to you things like, meet me downstairs in five minutes? I didn't think I was flirting *per se*. Frankie thought I was definitely flirting, and awkwardly at that. But it wasn't like that. It was just, when I carried around the things you sent me, things you had seen had thought had tasted had touched, things collected from your dreams which as we all know are as real as things that actually happened, I felt I was holding something so intensely real and loud and alive that I couldn't believe you, you were not here. I turned around a corner and really believed you would just materialize. Just like that. I couldn't believe you were not here with me.

I was standing next to a table when I decided to put away my phone for a few moments because I was feeling that something was, again, dying without my participation. People around me were all wearing red, which finally reminded me what this day meant, or was supposed to mean. On the table were steamed fish and meatballs in soy sauce and sweet and sour pork ribs and chicken soup and sticky rice pudding and all kinds of elaborate dishes. Frankie was perched on the arm of a couch, talking to some guy, laughing from time to time, punching him in the shoulder from time to time. Right in front of me were those fried spring rolls with red bean paste inside. I ate one after another. Spring rolls that started with a crunch and ended with explosive oil in my mouth. Sugared oil. The abundance made me sad, the too much of it all. Too much noise. Too much red. Too much oil. Too much of a feigned sociality rooted in some tradition that was so far removed from us, spatially and spiritually. Too much space occupied by others who I knew I would never understand. My heart ached at each tiny pause in the conversation, when I could sense that my interlocutor was scrambling for things to say, feeling more and more defeated as that pause went longer and longer, while in fact it couldn't have lasted for longer than half a second. We drank wine from paper cups and exchanged things of no value.

I fed myself another spring roll as the person in front of me finally found something to talk about: his shattered dreams. Voilà. I had discovered, for a while now, that I seemed to be in possession of some quality that would inevitably induce my interlocutor to talk about their shattered dreams. I wondered what that quality was. Perhaps, when he saw me standing there, wearing something decidedly out of place and chewing a crunchy spring roll without much grace, he was reminded of other deeply disappointing things. I reminded him of the gap between what he had probably imagined this night would be like and how it ended up looking. I felt some sympathy for him. So I listened. I was listening, but not entirely, since I was also thinking about an essay I read that morning. An essay by Adam Phillips titled *Desiring by Myself.* I made highlights throughout the essay with four different colors I remember: yellow, green, purple, and blue. When I started doing that I thought I had some kind of system, that these colors denoted different modes of engagement with the text, but by the end of it I no longer remembered which was which. By the end of it I was crying by myself. Weeping, in fact, which was worse. It was embarrassing, weeping over an essay, an essay that started out, as is often the case with Phillips, with a somewhat facetious tone, a proclamation that *most people feel guilty about masturbation*, because, as Leo Bersani once said, *they fear that masturbation is the truth about sex.* From then on it went downhill very quickly. Phillips went on to say that we never fall in love with an entire person, that what we love is what is absent, what we love is the aftermath of the object. To desire is to be left out. That we are just kidding ourselves when we ascribe the dimension of sociality to desiring, that there is always this gap between our solitary musings and the real objects we see in everyday life. *It's not to say, however, that reality is disappointing; it is that desire is excessive. It is not that we lack things; it is just that there are things that we want.* For an instant I thought the guy who was talking to me, I still didn't know his name, was going to cry too. I remembered he had been talking about wanting to get into academia but not being able to afford it, as if it were some luxurious good.

After reading the essay, I remember, I immediately sent it to you.

You read the first page and told me that Phillips made some good points.

Some good points.

Your words were few and countable this day because you were shooting a film

a short film about narcissism and self-pity. I envied that film.

I envied the creation.

I bit my lower lip as I read once again what you wrote:

He made some good points.

I would still be biting my lower lip when, later on, I traversed the entire campus to meet with my thesis advisor, in whose warm office I would always be allowed to feel better, that I could almost be led to believe that if I really wanted to, I could even *be* better. In his office I'd observe his hands—he used to be a hand model in his youth and I would suppress my urge to gauge the commercial value of his hands—and I'd choose my words carefully. I didn't have to. He would forgive anything. He had forgiven it all before I even made the mistake. He would even forgive my indecisiveness and my self-doubt, I was sure of that. On one of the rainy days he had told me, in quite an off-hand way, that there was something *fearless* in my writing. Later on, at a cocktail party with all the professors in our department, he described me, again in an off-hand way, as a *resilient* writer. To this day *fearless* and *resilient* are my two favorite words. I would always remember how he said them, with his enabling, magnanimous voice. His tenderness was unbearable. When he said those words I wanted to die on the spot so that I wouldn't do anything later on in this troublesome life that would offer him an opportunity to take them back. I wanted those words to stay even at the expense of my experience, or even my existence. Once I watched him walk his dog in Raleigh. One of those days with that typical apocalyptic weather, around November 2016. He was wearing his famous pin printed with the words *I love brains*. I caught a glimpse of him while he was walking his dog. Frankie and I were only in that town because we were trying to find some pizza-flavored ice-cream. And because that was our mission I felt ashamed when I saw him, walking his dog, not knowing that his fearless and resilient student was lusting for things cheesy and morose. No wait you are turning him into a god, Frankie said. But how could I not? If I didn't turn him into a god how could I even begin to put things on paper? If it isn't an offering it isn't worth anything. He wasn't aware of any of it of course—he was just walking his dog, deep in thought, deep in other thoughts, entirely on his own, as if he and his dog were the last two inhabitants on earth. An image that belongs on the back of a faded postcard that I would begin to carry around wherever I go, to remind myself that a god sometimes has a human face, and sometimes he walks his dog. I would hate myself if I misused a word with him. I'd hate to waste his time. I'd hate to waste his breaths. So there I would be, rushing towards my advisor's office while rehearsing in my mind the precise words I would present to him, even though I would remember we were both obsequious towards and doubtful of words. The emptiness. The emptiness that made me sick to my core. *He made some good points.* I chewed that sentence back and forth like a cow. I knew it was stupid. I hadn't eaten all day.

[Notes - Chapter on History]

Discussing fat pornography as a novel category, Don Kulick poses the question: "So, what's with the eating?"[5] My question is, "what's with the #eating?"

The hashtag, omnipresent, rapidly becomes "the first letter of your name, your home city, and every retrievable detail of your existence, whether you write it or not."[6]

An ever-expanding square with arms ever-stretching, transcending geographical borders and removing ideological differences

through an imagined connectivity

through the shared experience of looking at the same picture that

signals and enables the circulation of a virtual product

and, in the case of #foodporn, one that is subject to a diffusive and fundamentally pornographic gaze.

The essential limit of our desire is concretized in this sign, with a hole in it, whose emptiness is the emblem of everything we ever want.

Everything we ever want. And how pompous is that? I drank and drank my wine to swallow it all down, while it was determined to eat me up, upstream. When people are by themselves they have very strange thoughts, that's what Phillips said.

---

5   Don Kulick, "Porn," in *Fat: The Anthropology of an Obsession*, eds. Don Kulick and Anne Meneley (New York: Penguin, 2005), 85.

6   Benjamin Burdick, "#Hashtag," *Log* 30 (Winter 2014), 67.

And when they have very strange thoughts they write the best books. At the same time, that philosophical solitude is often associated with the emergence of desire, so, naturally, we would find solace in the company of others, because they either distract us or convince us that our self-doubt is not very serious. It doesn't make you very hopeful, does it, to view sociality, or the common life, in that way? My advisor would look at me. Well, not really at *me*. He would be looking at some non-entity floating in mid-air between us. He would say, this essay, I've noticed over the years, is one of those that folks feel compelled to send to friends after they read it. Yes, I would say, yes, yes, I guess that means after all we are not always *doing it alone*? Or perhaps I just wish we weren't. You're so right he would say, the essay seems to compel the performance of a kind of sociality or social bond whose naturalized existence the argument puts into question. I would think, yes, just like then, when I stood at the center of a party and the party was getting away from me. I was listening to the academic-wanna-be, his eyes weirdly cutting and weirdly misty, and trying to convince myself that really it was me he wanted to talk to at this precise moment, and what he was saying to me then was the most important thing in the world that touched the core of our being. I shifted the entire weight of my being onto the act of listening. I would have liked to reach out to him. Yes. I moved my eyeballs like they were little cameras trying to capture the tiny muscles moving around his eyes and his mouth. I dissected his words and paid particular attention to the ellipses, because that's the most important thing isn't it, the things we leave unsaid. While listening to him I realized someone else was looking at this picture of us, me listening, him talking. I could feel moist attention falling on my skin like raindrops.

I cast a seemingly casual glance in that direction and saw the looker, a vaguely good-looking person, in a different corner of the room. I wondered if they would make their way across the room in their black shirt with their collar wide open. Then I turned my attention back to the guy who was talking at me. I'd hoped to understand a thing or two about his fears and hopes and dreams, but at the same time I felt the futility of my sacrificial ineptitude, as he went on and on about objects I didn't own and symbolic systems I couldn't share. At one point the guy might have done something, like putting his hand on my shoulder or at least somewhere really close to my hair. I wasn't sure. I thought briefly about that other person who had been looking at us, who still hadn't walked over, hadn't introduced themselves, hadn't made the mistake of introducing themselves. I imagined what they would say to me and what I would say in response. The colors of the gestures they never made and the weight of the words they had never placed on the table. This almost felt like happiness, this moment when nothing had happened, when nothing had been irrevocably said, and everything was still possible, like the pause between one sentence and the next, like a train that never arrived. In that interval spring had come and gone and summer was here, all absent-minded. It occurred to me that those things that could happen but didn't were also part of the history of our desires.

I was turning into all kinds of liquids. Droplets of cold sweat gathered on my forehead around midnight. Blood never stopped flowing out of my body, long and quiet. Come to think of it, in human porn, for lack of a better word, the money shot always comes with liquids, bursting out, rushing out, contaminating the lenses, contaminating our perception, while in food porn the money shot is the luscious sauce that coats the pasta in a sensuous light, the glorious goo that soaks the sandwich bread, an egg yolk that thickens just so perfectly, creating a creamy, unctuous ooze which, when finally released from its surrounding body, rushes out and makes everything it touches golden and good. There is nothing like forking a good yolk into submission, wrote one food blogger. Oh the rupture, the intrusion, the sense of relief, of liberation. When I forked open such a good egg Frankie and I were at a nice restaurant called Littler. As March began, we went to a nice restaurant almost every evening, eating dish after dish of the remains of cold animals drenched in sauces made from a green pulp of mashed vegetables and garnished with edible little flowers, all grown in the chef's back garden, naturally. It was ridiculous, really, in retrospect, to live a life that was barely affordable. We must have thought, at the time, that these moments might be so-called eventful when we began to have time, later on, to recollect them. But while we were eating up our days like that we were also nourishing the fear that it might not be the case. That all of this would just be as blurry and weightless as the smoke enveloping us. Something would add up eventually, sums, or substances stuck to the inner walls of our organs. *That* we vaguely knew, but at the time, when we were still reveling in what these things did to our tongues and lungs, those practical considerations were just problems for the future self we had no interest in, and would never need to apologize to, at least not face-to-face. As the night progressed we would end up several blocks away in a wine lounge or cocktail bar, handing the number we got from one guy to another, taking selfies, lots, without sending them to anyone, initially. And one night, one of the guys we met introduced us to vaping. He showed us how you put your mouth to a USB-shaped thing and suck on it. Life begins with sucking, after all. I didn't tell him that, of course.

I did tell you about this observation, I believe, and you laughed (I imagined, or at least smiled) and said, good pun.

As the vaping guy was still doing that—sucking, suckling—I remembered again what Freud once said about men who never get out of the oral stage: they become epicures in kissing. Or else they become heavy drinkers and smokers. Yes he did use the word *epicure*, or the German equivalent. I wondered what women would become, by that logic. Neon lights flashed on the face of this man who was tangibly losing himself in purely chemical indulgence. Frankie watched him with some concern. She frowned and said, this is kinda weird not gonna lie. She said she still preferred real cigarettes. At least you know what's in there.

After saying goodbye to the man with the fake cigarettes, we sat on the curb next to the bar to smoke our real ones. Chocolate-flavored ones that would unfailingly leave that bittersweet fragrance on our fingertips afterwards. At one point a middle-aged white man walked by and shouted at us for sitting there smoking. It was decadent, according to him. At another point Frankie was saying to me, someone asked me about you, you know. Who? Oh just some guy from that Chinese New Year party last week. Okay, I said. Frankie looked down at the ashes that were scattered around her shoes. Then she said, oh never mind, I think what he was trying to do was to plant some idea in you *through me*, and you know that really isn't my thing, so I won't tell you who that is. I nodded and thanked her, but at the same time I felt that indeed, he might have succeeded in planting some idea in me in a sinuous way. Is it weird if I feel a bit good about it? No of course not Frankie said, it's always nice to be seen, but you can't be so easily influenced. She said that while we were both gladly influenced by nicotine. I put my head on her shoulder and she rested hers against mine. That was always nice. As our cigarettes came to an end Frankie asked me what was going on with the film guy. I said nothing much, really, we're just texting a lot. What is a lot Frankie asked. Yeah I said, probably like 8 a.m. to 4 a.m. Fuck, Frankie said, as she killed her cigarette against the curb. She seemed to be considering this commitment. After a while she finally asked, so let's be real, are you going to sleep with him or not? The question was so shocking that immediately I had to cough. I wanted to press the unhear button that must be hidden somewhere. After failing to find the button I began to explain to her, no, you see... but then I felt something rising, surging, bulging like an abominable bad dream involving green-blue apocalyptical waves closing in from every direction and the scariest thing was that this apocalypse seemed to be happening right inside of me. So I said to her, wait, wait, I think I'm going to throw up.

I did it in one of the small alleys, against the brick wall. It was so disgusting I was immediately ashamed. I wondered why processed food is something we find disgusting, even when it has been processed by our own inner chambers. This. This had been inside me, I remember thinking. I wondered whether it had something to do with privacy, because, turning my gaze away from what I created while still feeling the remnants of that sickness, it did feel like I was being turned inside out. I was walking back to Frankie inside out, with faulty organs I couldn't quite name hanging loosely from my torso. Can she see I'm actually all messed up with the wrong side out? I could hear the sound of the wind as it traveled through the hollow corridors that used to connect one thing to another but were at that moment in disarray.

While I was still finding my way back to Frankie I got a few texts from you. You were describing a bad year of yours. Actually, this year is pretty bad too, you said. During that bad year you found out you were depressed and you freaked out. It turned out that freaking out about depression is even worse than depression itself. I came to a sudden stop near the exit of the little alley, near the visible edge between light and shadows. I stood there, contemplating your words. Everyone was depressed those days, including my ex-boyfriend who left me for pretty boys. One day this ex-boyfriend told me that it crushed him when he found out what he took to be metaphysical pain was simply physical depression. To have believed, at one point,that his pain was singular and unprecedented must have provided some solace. Then he said, you know, I always hate anyone who is reading the same book I'm reading. When I was in Rome, walking those old streets made of stone,

I hated all the people, generations and generations of people, who once walked those same streets. The existence of others renders everything we do inevitably vulgar. As long as there are others, we can never be saved. Is that so, I had asked, quite astonished at all of this. But just then I thought I could understand. I leaned against the wall and sat down. The street was also made of stone. Cold and impartial. On my cold screen you were still describing your depression, your depression looking like a devil, sweating and grinning, lurking in a corner.

But you couldn't understand it, you had treated life very well.

You had always been nice to life but life still fucked up your heart.

You were asking me why it should be like this
why was it that sadness to you
was knowledge and not
a feeling.

Meanwhile the coolness of the stone was climbing up my spine and various liquids were climbing up my esophagus, asking me to hey, hey, don't say anything. I began to type with two fingers. It was nice that my fingers were untainted. I typed quickly. I quoted some Virginia Woolf that I thought might be comforting, until I remembered Virginia Woolf had many many bad years.

Then I waited, occasionally placing my phone face-down on my lap, until a message finally popped up and in the message you said you believed we now almost hit the mark where we should suspend this online conversation until further in-person contact.

Why is that, may I ask?

Meanwhile, the acidic aftertaste resurfaced, with tepid regret.

You replied that you were afraid you didn't have
much life left to share with me.

I considered this. Then I might have said
but you see, we probably will never see each other in person.

You replied quickly. You said, but probability
is a man-made thing.

Then you told me you were walking in the snow, while currents of fickle warmth pierced through your abdomen like needles, sewing up all your not-yet-thought thoughts. *You must know everything*, I suddenly thought. I wasn't sure what I meant by that. *Either* I believed you should have already known all of it, you, all sewed-up like a patch doll, you must already know everything, things for which I didn't even have the proper names. Before I was able to formulate the questions you already have all the answers. *Or*, it could mean, I must tell you everything, like you prophesied. For instance I must tell you about this moonlight dripping through me as if I were an orphan well. I must tell you about this stone dissolving beneath me. There is nothing you shouldn't know.

And then you said, we can always increase the probability.

I considered this again, this time with greater effort. Before I could reply you said something else entirely irrelevant, something about a dried daffodil you picked up on the way. It was just like you, to say something that was mildly seductive to be followed by some poetic nonsense. You entirely broke the rules of contextual reading. I was at a loss. But because it didn't add up, I believed there must be some hidden meaning. Somewhere. There had to be. Some meaning that preferably involves me. I just have to be a more careful reader.

Frankie was calling my name from the other side asking if I was okay.

Yes, I shouted back.

I read your words again. I imagined you walking, stopping, picking up a dried up daffodil on the way. I imagined you walking down a dark hallway. You were returning to your room. Your room consisted only of the objects you described to me: your heater, your books, your whiskey. You walked into your bare room with only those items around and you returned to the topic of probability. Then you were telling me again that it was a man-made thing, and you said it again, but see, we can always increase the probability.

I said to you, please don't get my hopes up.

And you said, why.

I said, I might not make an effort.

Who would, you said.

In my phone notes were these folders: *Bits of Writing*, *Dreams*, *Recipes*, and *Things That Make Me Puke*. The last list went: Cuban sandwich, shrimp tempura, tequila shots, bacon burger, Cheetos. And the next day, during my nine o' clock seminar, I added to the list: the USB-thingy. Perhaps the USB-thingy plus five French 75's. Frankie was right. It's dangerous because we don't know what's in there. The German guy sitting in front of me was wearing a gray beanie today and for some reason I couldn't stop looking at it and counting the threads of yarn. The professor was saying, in his plaintive voice, that style is the intrusion of the body into language. An individualization of the body. The story will evolve in the pursuit of language. Well, in fact, all styles are exhausted now. Does that mean all bodies are exhausted, I wanted to ask. I didn't.

After class I opened the door to the last winter day and saw a flower near the pavement, a little pink flower, rolling in the grass. A flower that was entirely free. Free because it would never be picked up by someone or used to adorn someone's windowsill, notebook, or lapel, because it was already uprooted, carried around by the levity of the wind. The flower rolled happily past the sidewalk, down the curb, onto the asphalt, until it was flattened by some tires eventually. I thought of you when I saw that flower, perhaps because of how free and sad it was, but I didn't tell you that, because I remembered how you said, *who would*.

In the new cafeteria that looked like the headquarters of some startup, with green sectional couches and giant glass windows, I got an iced coffee while I texted Frankie. Then I sat next to one window and looked out. In this part of the world people dressed simply. Sweatshirts and leggings and sneakers and basketball caps and black backpacks. The lack of originality in these visual elements intrigued me. Nothing seemed to differentiate one object (or subject?) from the next, but somehow we'd be able to find one smile, one gait, one scent, that we allow ourselves to fall for. I sipped my coffee and thought about what you told me. A common goal. To desire in installments. I wondered when you said *common* do you mean *shared* or do you mean *typical*. I returned to my screen. I read the captions from all the Instagram food posts hashtagged #foodporn. *Please deliver to my bed ASAP*; *Balls are my weakness, juicy af* (talking about lamb meatballs); *Let's naked this* (Freudian slip?); *This Hungry Hoe needs some soup for her soul, a bowl of ramen fills up the hole; Orgasmi di prima mattinaaa.* All these images had one thing in common, the visual hallmark of pornographic aesthetic: the extreme close-up. The way the hairs on a kiwi fruit stand up in the light like the fine hairs on someone's neck. Or the way a piece of sashimi leans inside a bed of flowers, bathed in dim candlelight. The rawness itself is provocative. I felt uncomfortably close to the action. Then I wanted to get even closer. My lips were dry and I sipped my coffee again. I began to write on the back of a menu:

[Notes on Chapter on Food and Desire]

We are doomed to never get enough food, because the prototypical feeding, together with the satisfaction it promises, is at the same time always failing us.

In his notoriously difficult essay "Femininity," Freud notes that girls reproach their mothers not only for not giving them a penis, but also for giving them too little milk ("Femininity," 122).

Building upon this idea, Melanie Klein distinguishes the "good breast" from the "bad breast." In her account, the infant will hold a perpetual grudge against the breast that deprives him, which, at the point of separation, becomes bad because it keeps the milk, love, and care associated with the good breast all to itself. ("Envy and Gratitude," 42.)

In both accounts, a hunger is produced and perpetuated by its very insatiability.

The description that the infant feels deprived presupposes an aspiration for wholeness and completeness.

A promise is given that is, once again, always accompanied by a sense of loss, which impresses the infant, and later the grownup, with the unattainability of complete satisfaction.

I looked up from my screen and spotted Frankie in the crowd. She was wearing a green shirt, the green of young leaves. While she was still walking towards me I made an effort to pull myself back into the scene. Frankie, my only anchor in reality. When she was standing right in front of me the first question she asked was if I had eaten anything yet. No I said. She said she hadn't either and would probably just get a big smoothie. Sounds good I said.

Frankie turned around and headed for the juice bar. I was about to write again when a blonde girl in a pink cap with Greek letters walked by, gave me a glance but soon took the glance back. A touch and not yet a touch, but far less poetic than that. I looked down at my screen and sipped my coffee. Two summers ago the blonde girl and I shared a room when we were doing an internship together. My entire memory of that room was of her pacing back and forth in front of the television telling me about her Tinder dates and me writing things down into my journal unrelated to her Tinder dates. We were doing the internship in a foreign city on a different continent. We didn't know anyone else. So we had to talk to each other. In all the coffee shops of that foreign city she showed me pictures of her family and her dog, her cousin's wedding, her ski trips. I praised everything, but maybe I shouldn't have. During weekends she asked me to accompany her to the boutiques on main street where I sat in a majestic chair and she tried on colorful blouses. She would be pouting in front of the mirror and saying to me, ugh, what do you think? Looks amazing I said, you are a walking catalog. She smiled at me in the mirror. I wasn't sure how her usual friends would handle the situation, whether they would be standing very close to her and offering more in-depth comments, or whether they would stay rather nonchalant, sinking into that majestic chair talking about men and looking utterly uninterested in the sight of her in a blouse that had way too many colors. I wouldn't know. Sometimes we went to the beach and she would just stand there and watch the waves for the entire afternoon, while I wrote. She would say, hey, you know what, I used to write too. Yeah? I said. Then I feel there's nothing much to write about she said. Her pale blonde hair would dance in the wind as she laughed about her old hobby. Her pale blonde hair suited her new hobbies very well but her roots were showing. Neither of us ate very much, but still we were obsessed with the food markets, the steamed dumplings the honey fudges the frikkadels. We did other things too. We went to parks, wine tastings, galleries, and the day when *Obergefell* was decided we went to a bar called *Yours Truly* to celebrate. I always hated that expression because the people who refer to themselves as *yours truly* are usually neither *true* nor *yours*, they are just messing with you for nothing. She was in a good mood that day. Perhaps the decision reminded her of where she came from and how great it was to come from there, I guess. It was a cold June and we sat on the terrace. She drank Riesling and said to me, here's a secret: if you drink enough, just enough and not too much, you wouldn't feel hungry for a long time. Interesting I said. I observed the mountain in the distance. Darkness was about to get thicker. Then she said, how lucky we are to be alive right now. I turned to look at her. At the time this was not yet a famous line from a hit musical. So I was stunned. I suspected it was something she would never say if she were with her real friends. At one point that evening a guy walked all the way from the other end of the terrace just to compliment the dress I was wearing, while we both knew very well he was trying to talk to her, not me, and he just didn't know how to get to her. I thanked him politely while she smiled into the dusk. When he finally left she began to giggle and she said, eww. Before we left the city we made plans to still get coffee and hang out after we got back to campus. A year and a half later she was walking past me in the cafeteria, oblivious, unperturbed, heading straight to some other girls who were waiting for her next to those green sectionals. They were all blonde and bony and would always know what was expected of them.

I picked up my phone again and saw a few messages from you. You were cold, you told me, and it was raining outside

and it was the closest you'd come to being in love in the last several months.

I wanted to ask you oh really, you are capable of being in love?, but instead I asked if you could smell that smell in the air when it was just about to rain and the clouds were scheming overhead.

Yes you said, and you were reading a book with the rain hitting on your window panes this very moment

and you said reading it was like drinking moonshine

on a completely frozen street.

I like this simile, I said, I really like it.

Alcohol is warm, you said, but we choose to drink it cold.

Frankie was back with her smoothie the green of young leaves. It had a label that read *Green Goddess*. She took a sip of her Green Goddess and started brainstorming where we would end up that night, someone's house or the only club in town. At the same time she showed me pictures from other people's Instagram and commented on the drama behind the scenes. Beautiful girls and their insecurities. Over boys, looks, connections, money. Their secret attractions to one another. Their jealousies. Interesting I said. Don't you sometimes just wish you were a white person, Frankie said, everything would be so simple. Like what? I asked. We were walking now, walking vaguely towards something, I wasn't sure what. Our sense of destination was flimsy and dull. We had to keep walking around like this, aimlessly, all these hopeless, intoxicated evenings, until the sky meanly whitened, until our blood was full of cheap wine and our wine glasses full of cheap smiles. There, we would find ourselves trapped in a familiar scene of bodies in music, music in bodies, with Frankie telling me over cigarette smoke and drum beats that I held this visible contempt for men so that even though they found me attractive they never approached me. Or maybe she said *even if* and not *even though*. Is that so I asked. Or maybe I asked is that so obvious. I probably still hadn't eaten anything when the night was beginning to melt at our fingertips, when it felt like someone was shoving their hand into my stomach trying to find a ring or a locket they lost there. I looked around. Some girl was wailing loudly at a corner of this balcony, her makeup streaming down and her face looking like an abstract painting. Some glasses or beer bottles were being smashed. More people were taking selfies that would soon be sent to a select few. On the table were pizzas and chicken fingers and chips dipped in hummus, all looking violently at me. Threatening gazes from a half-eaten pizza, huh. How did we end up here? Sometimes entire blocks of time passed me by without me noticing. How did we put on makeup and lingered in front of her mirror? How did Frankie dance on her balcony and count her trees again while smoking one of her very last cigarettes? How did I stroll in her living room with a glass of wine in my hand admiring the image of myself with a glass of wine in my hand wearing things stolen from Frankie's wardrobe? No wonder we dressed alike. I took another drag and listened again to Frankie talk about people. Beautiful people who had to keep doing things to prove that they were beautiful, like indiscriminately sleeping with others. I looked into Frankie's eyes. I asked her what was going on with the free-association guy, or, Donut? I made certain to mention them both. Frankie rolled her eyes and said oh you see I'm never approaching these things the way you do. How do *I* do it I asked. She said well you are really intense. She said you think too much. She said perhaps you could try and live a little lighter. Then she blew out a perfect smoke ring, laughed.

At the breakfast table I was sitting with people from my country. They were saying, wow you look really tired. They said it nicely so I couldn't really complain or protest. They had with them on the breakfast table thick textbooks of macroeconomics or statistics or organic chemistry but they didn't seem overwhelmed by their weight at all. In fact they seemed very content with the presence of those tomes because you see they had an enormous appetite and they wanted much much more. After all, they had been promised as much. They stuffed their plates with biscuits and gravy and bloody cakes at eight in the morning. Mouthfuls and mouthfuls of red velvet. They were still so easily impressed by the abundance of food. Who could blame them. The generosity of appetite, a generosity that permits us to carry on living. Everything was going really, really well, was the gist of their conversation. We'd all have bright futures, as long as we keep biting off more than we can chew.

After breakfast I sat down on the steps in front of the chapel. The sun was harsh enough that dust in the air shimmered. Everything was glistening under the sun. People's faces. A universal sparkle. Many years later I would discover it was right in front of this chapel that a scene from a famous film was shot where a woman was hanged for stepping out of line. The hanged woman was even played by an alum, I believe. I had no idea why the school would ever allow an image like that to be associated with its most iconic building, but again, this was a campus where, during my sophomore year, a noose was found on a tree. But back then I had no idea, oblivious to all that I was sitting in front of the chapel and squinting under a splendid sun to read your messages. Back then I was only thinking about the significance of the sun that was all over us. Too much sun, in fact. We had never seen so much sun. Stubborn sun. Sun that would be squeezing all the water out of our bodies. Our bodies like pillars of salt. I went back to you under the sun. You repeatedly claimed you would suspend this conversation. You kept talking to me. You gave me your word until words like *before*, *when*, and *after* lost their meanings. I quite liked that. I wish I could tell you what it felt like, a conversation with no beginning and no end, where nothing is ever forgotten. In that ever-flowing and over-flowing conversation we were both waiting for something to happen, I knew. Many times I thought something would happen very soon. Perhaps the next second. All the times when you said, oh you. Oh. You. I lay down on the grass and heard all kinds of birdsong. I saw very big clouds. Some people believed spring was truly, undeniably here and a spring market was assembled. Hand-made jewelry and cute little porcelain cups and food trucks among other curiosities. I thought about that season in Shanghai stuck between spring and summer. The best season, when spring and summer were still fighting it out with the scent of rain and perpetual struggle in the air that really couldn't be found anywhere else. I told you about it and you began to give me vignettes of that city, of the sycamore trees, dust in the spring air, soup from street vendors, still hot and bubbly, the smell of watermelon in every small alley during the monsoon season, and those Shikumen neighborhoods, formidable brick walls and delicate colonial houses, cemented balconies with pots of gardenia, grape vines meandering from one stone gate to another, and tiled roofs with many, many pigeons. I wondered who still lived in one of those houses. You lived in such a house as a kid, before the age of cellphones, when you could easily disappear into a shadow around the corner of a staircase and no one would bother you with text messages or emails or calls, no one would even know where you were and they never cared to know. I never lived in a place like that. Sometimes you talked about what happened in that city like someone talking about a victory that does not belong to him, or a love that is doomed to fail. The city I never knew.

I was breathing in the scent of freshly cut grass when
I saw another message from you. A poem.
I read it several times and recognized the poem.
I felt slightly disoriented. Breathe, I told myself,
breathe, breathe. So you were, you had confessed
in a poem, giving yourself to me in pieces.
What do I do with them? I asked. And you said,
do whatever you like with them. They are all yours. Oh
god,
I thought, aren't we being too dramatic?
I paused, breathed again, tried to figure out whether I ate anything at breakfast (did I?), but couldn't really perform any of those thought activities starting with re-. I had to put you away for a while. I lit a cigarette. By this point I'd had thousands of cigarettes but the one I was smoking that day was different from all others, blazing, dazing. It was incredibly good. I could feel how the smoke traveled through my entire body and knocked on doors to various organs and how the lobes, hearing that call,

were jittering with buoyant merriment.

When Frankie found me I probably had a dreamlike expression on my face because her first reaction was, oh come on, what did he say this time. I couldn't tell her anything when she frowned like that. I knew she would be incredulous and that would break me a little. There are many things we can't really explain to others, not even our best friends. Like our dreams. Like the fact that I knew you were giving yourself to me in pieces but I didn't know what to do with them. So I just said to her, hmm, gelato? Yeah sure she said. We each got a gelato from one of the food trucks. I got vanilla and she had coffee. We sat and ate our gelato. For a moment everything was creamy and sweet and melting at the roof of our palates and the corner of our eyes. Frankie seemed happy, so happy that she began to tell that story again, the story of how we first met. Do you remember that? Oh yes, I said, you keep reminding me. It was almost four years ago. We were the first two international students to arrive on campus and were sent to a dorm building that felt like a prison. Only the two of us in the entire building and the walls seemed to be closing in. I had no linens or pillows or anything so I placed my head on a folded jacket. I had nobody to talk to and nothing to do so I decided to fall asleep as quickly as I could. In the middle of the night someone knocked on my door. Frankie had crawled all the way down the empty hallway just to knock on my door and tell me, someone she didn't know yet, that she was afraid. Of what? I had allegedly said. I don't know, Frankie had said, it's so empty in here. Is that so? I had allegedly said. Frankie immediately recognized me as this incredibly cold person, and we all know first impressions are nearly impossible to shake off. She crawled back to her own room and for the entire first year we didn't have further interactions. She mentioned she would run into me each night in the lobby of our dorm. That, I do remember. I remember seeing her hurriedly going out in impeccable makeup when I was coming back from the gym all sweaty and faded, in my green sneakers and khaki jacket and one of those free t-shirts you could never get too many of as a first-year. We nodded to each other in a cursory sort of way. We were not friends yet. Sometimes we imagined the other's life. A good life. It must be. But what she didn't know was that I had been living on yogurt and blueberries for three months and running for three hours a day. I had no idea why I did that. I never really liked blueberries. I hated running. The emptiness I felt was so enormous I couldn't conceive that another person I nodded at in the lobby would be feeling the same way.

Another thing I didn't tell her—and I don't believe I ever told anyone—was something that happened one day on my way back from the gym. I had a yogurt in my hand and was walking in near darkness thinking about my readings, feeling weak and alert, as people often do after sweating. As I was still thinkingabout the famous Laura Mulvey essay I just read, a voice came from behind. The voice of a man. He was saying, excuse me, excuse me. Yes? I turned to face him. Under the streetlight he was terribly white, his blond hair disheveled and his hands in the pockets of his sport jacket. I didn't know why it struck me so, his whiteness. As he approached I took a tiny step back. He took another step forward. He smiled. He said he had been noticing me and he just wanted to say he liked me very much. At first I listened. I think I really gave out the impression of someone listening and trying to understand, which is unfortunate. Because soon, in the shadows behind him some other people began to emerge, who were chuckling very lightly, each whiter than the next. It occurred to me then that really whiteness is a feeling. Sometimes not a good feeling. I was still holding onto my yogurt and recognizing from their laughter that this was either a Truth or Dare or a task some fraternity gave to new pledges. Even with that insight I couldn't think of anything to say. I was swaying a bit in the wind and my khaki jacket was turning into a smudge of oblivion in this night scene. At least that's how it felt like. During those few seconds the guy in front of me was still doing his best to look sincere but there were those ridiculous sparks in his eyes. Colder than moonlight. I had two sleevefuls of wind. You really believed that, his eyes seemed to be saying, you really believed what you just heard? There was so much wind that I was turning into a balloon. I turned around and began to walk away. Apart from the wind that was filling me up it was an otherwise tranquil night. He was still saying things at my back when I was already walking away. That terrifying insistence. No but you have to listen. Why do I have to? Asking another person to listen is probably the most presumptuous ask in the world.

I had no idea why this episode resurfaced then, then of all times, in the middle of a perfectly serene gelato-eating scene on the first day of spring. Probably because my gelato was melting and beginning to look a lot like yogurt. I stirred it with my plastic spoon, round and round. Yogurt could never be a food porn star. It's too innocent-looking, too healthy, too white. You'd need to be a bit colorful and exotic to be sexualized.

We picked ourselves up from the grass and began walking. Walking on grass but sadly not barefoot. Frankie was leading the way to some hidden reading room she was eager to show me.

She had written her best pages there. She was wearing a watermelon-colored dress, exposing some portions of her back. A few minutes later, we would end up on the top floor of the library tower, a hidden room, which looked like where Rapunzel might have lived. I would pace around the circular room and think about that famous Edgar Allan Poe story about a cell just like this one, with a pit and a pendulum. My worst nightmare. Frankie would sit down at the only desk in the center of everything typing away as if she were telling me that see, Rapunzel, you have to write your way out. She would keep on typing. I would lean at the window, watch her with fascination, trying to learn. But not then. Then you were still texting me. You texted me. You texted me just to tell me you saw the Devil again today. Meanwhile I was treading on freshly cut grass, taking in words from you and Frankie at the same time. I felt a small numbness in my chest, like some part very close to the heart had been anesthetized. I determined that this discomfort, too, should be metaphysical. I thought about whether I should tell you that, while you were going on and on about a flower pinned to the Devil's button— the Devil was late today, alas. I bit my lips. You empathize too much, Frankie said, you don't always have to.

And this metaphysical discomfort can be soothed by looking, it seemed. I printed out images of #foodporn and pinned them to my board. I stared and stared at those images, of a mac-and-cheese sandwich flashing me with its enticing, undisguised interior, of a shiny orange glistening showing off its luster, of a languid egg yolk coyly giving me the eye from a cozy nest of linguine. Unlike human porn that relies on temporal narration and gradual buildup of tension, in #foodporn we only get the grand finale. Occasionally, there will be an appropriate dose of fabricated culinary foreplay, such as a satisfying ketchup squeeze. Occasionally, a fork, a bite, or a finger in the frame tempts us to identify with the imaginary *eater* and anticipate the next move. We leer and drool and wonder what they will do next and how far they will go. But generally we are spared all that. What we want and what we get is the ultimate, the timeless, the idealized beautiful world where syrup is always drizzling, ice-cream always melting, and sauce always pouring. Always. We don't know and we don't want to know that sometimes milk can be glue, blemishes on strawberries can be covered up by lipsticks, and pancakes can be stacked up by hidden cardboards. We'd rather not know so that we can look some more. Sometimes staring at these pictures I'd think about what would happen if I started eating them. There was a time when I did eat paper. Books. Books are the best because the ink is often good. It would be another few years before I read a case study where another girl said she enjoyed eating paper. This girl was more peculiar. She only ate her mother's novels. A lot can be said about that. I googled *eat paper: What does it mean if you eat paper in your dream? Is it okay to eat paper when you are pregnant? Does eating paper kill you, and how quickly?* These are all very good questions, and it was reassuring that other people had been wondering about similar things. But I knew I could not eat these pictures on my board, raw materials for my project that I should save for another day. So I asked myself to be content with looking. I stared and stared at pictures of avocado, papaya, and passion fruit with the same rapture as those of éclair, sausage or aubergine. It pleased me a great deal that my desire did not seem to be entirely phallo-centric.

I sent several pages to the printer. Then I sat down at my desk and began to write to you.

I wrote to you a lot. Perhaps too much.

I wrote to you on good paper, sometimes

I'd scatter a few dried cherry blossom petals in the fat envelope.

I may have even sent out one

or two of those letters.

I may have even sent you a whiskey glass with a tiny Mount Fuji

at the bottom.

When I was writing this particular letter it occurred to me that March

was coming to an end. You had promised to write in March you see

but you never did.

I sat in front of my desk and thought about how pathetic it was that in all kinds of encounters we always keep this leger, recording what is received and what is given and I wished

I had the courage to be more prodigal with my feelings.

My roommate was profuse in that area. When I was staring at some insignificant thing on my desk, a post-it or a pen or something, she entered the room full of worrisome energy. Guess what, she said, I think I just met the love of my life. Congratulations, I said. My roommate really did look good. Amazing things love can do to one's colors. She was a tiny person and like all tiny persons she liked to act like a diva, pacing around like it was not her own room, like she was a queen inspecting her territories for the first time. Finally my roommate settled on my desk and said, oh, our meeting was just like a movie. You can't imagine how beautiful it was. What meeting? I asked. With the love of my life! She cried, have you been listening? Oh yes, sorry, I said, what about it. And there, she crossed her legs and began to give me this scene: so, she was reading in the coffee shop, it was a beautiful day out, (and by the way, she'd recommend I get out more,) and the moment she lifted her eyes from her book, he just walked in! They do that, I said. She ignored me and went into detail about how much she'd like to fuck him. There really were a lot of things she could do to him, and naturally, I thought, not that many things he could do to her. When she was done with all that she turned to ask me what about you do you have any men in your life recently? I said no not really. She said oh come on. And at that exact moment her phone rang. It rang and rang and rang. She said hang on and took a video-call right there in front of me and the voice of some guy was suddenly here in the room.It happened just like that and he was suddenly in the room with us.

Oh hey, he said. Hey how's it going she said. She giggled. Then they began saying a lot of things only because a third person was there in the room, was what it felt like. Wet and windy and sultry. Ah no, don't say that, she giggled. Aww you know that's not true. I flipped my page over loudly and began to write on the other side while my roommate giggled and giggled and giggled. A century later, when my roommate finally hung up, she sighed deeply and made a point that this was not the guy she most wanted to fuck. I nodded. Alright I see. She went back to describing the guy she most wanted to fuck while I opened our mini-fridge and took out a cookie dough.

Several hours later, when I walked into my advisor's office, the whole scene was drenched in rain. It felt like the room was raining and my soul was getting damper but in reality it was not even raining outside. My roommate was right. We had a plentiful sun that day. In front of our departmental building some people were playing some game with a football. I lowered my head so as not to be hit by the sun or the football. My advisor was hurriedly writing something down when I knocked on his open door, and he acknowledged my presence with the drop of his pen.How I liked that. I had usurped the pen. I said my greetings and handed my pages to him. He did not make eye contact, not immediately. He started reading, quickly and vehemently, his eyes moving from one line to the next. And while he was doing that I thought about you. A minute ago I had asked you how long you thought we could continue to talk like this, and you had told me, *as long as you like; as briefly as you like.* Moving from line to line my advisor coughed a small cough, which sounded like a big cough because of how quiet it all was. And then I saw it, I saw his lips silently forming words and phrases, which painfully reminded me that yes he was reading it, he was reading what I wrote and I suddenly felt very ashamed. It wasn't that I was unsure about my writing, no, I had long overcome that, but sitting there, when my words were at his fingertips and his lips, I felt he could tell from those pages that I had been distracted. That my fixation on one specific person had destroyed the purported universality of it all.

> Lacan links this sense of loss to the event of separation, tracing it back to the weaning period (severage), primarily designating the nursling's loss of the breast but also other crises caused by separation, particularly the expulsion from the mother's body at birth. The weaning—traumatizing or not—leaves an enduring psychical trace, the effects of which take precedence over any experiences of sexual repression.[7] We have never had enough milk, and we will never fulfill our sexual desires. This failure fits into Lacan's grander thesis that desire is sustainedthrough its lack of satisfaction, even its impossibility.[8] As virtually everyone in psychoanalysis would agree, desiring begins in the absence of the object—in the aftermath. Once the object is out of the picture—temporarily lost—desire begins.

> The loss is made up for by subsequent efforts to feed oneself; hence the loop: feeding—loss—feeding. According to Freud, in later developmental phases, the child attempts to renew the satisfaction from nourishment by thumb-sucking.

---

7   Shuli Barzilai, *Lacan and the Matter of Origins* (Stanford, CA: Stanford University Press, 1999), 22-4.

8   Jacques Lacan, *On Feminine Sexuality: The Limits of Love and Knowledge* (New York: Norton, 1998), 6.

In *Three Essays on the Theory of Sexuality*, he further claims that some of them, who do not detach completely from the erotogenic significance of the labial region, will become "epicures in kissing," or "if males, will have a powerful motive for drinking and smoking." Freud seems to suggest that for women, however, the intensified attachment manifests itself in the form of repression. He observes that "they will feel disgust at food and will produce hysterical vomiting."[9] He proceeds to give us an account of his women patients suffering from disturbances of eating, globus hystericus, constriction of the throat, and vomiting. Freud fails to address, however, why only men would become drinkers and kissers. In her book *What Lacan Said About Women*, Colette Soler entreats us to always remember to situate Freud's "scandalous phallic phase" in a specific historical moment of capitalism, where the social discrepancy between two sexes are translated into the unconscious. [10]

[...]

In the end, it is an image—a fantasy—that we are looking at. We are not actually eating. The dimension of the taste—the actual consumption—is only achieved through imagination, an imagination that is, to some extent, fuller, better.

---

9   Sigmund Freud, "Three Essays on the Theory of Sexuality," reprinted in *The Standard Edition of the Complete Psychological Works of Sigmund Freud, Volume VII* (1901-1905): *A Case of Hysteria, Three Essays on Sexuality and Other Works*, trans J. Strachey (London: Hogarth Press, 1948), 182.

10   Colette Soler, *What Lacan Said About Women*, trans. John Holland (New York: Other, 2006), 159.

As Anna Freud once remarked, "in your dreams you can have your eggs cooked the way you want them, but you can't eat them."[11] By presenting inedible food images and imbuing them with non-perishable qualities, #foodporn is an enabling absence; the promise of the pleasure is given, whilst the object of desire is already, forever, lost. It is enabling in the sense that it keeps us wanting (to see) more.

But he didn't point that out. When he finished reading he put down those pages gently and he said, you do realize your subject is a white female subject? The first time he made eye contact with me that day and I was crushed. Yes, I said, perhaps, but not intentionally. I said it feebly since I knew the un-intentionality made it worse. He looked away. His eyes landed on the spines of his books. Then he asked me if I ever considered whether there was something subversive in this phenomenon that wasnot personal or diffuse. Structurally, socially, what could it do? What could this desire do? He wasn't asking these questions too harshly, but with his usual tenderness and encouragement, personally, diffusely. I almost wanted to say, but what could it do, any of this, all of this? Please tell me what theory could possibly do, structurally, socially. But you see I couldn't really say that. It wasn't his fault, after all. It wasn't his fault that I was not entirely comfortable with these terms or with the terms of my own engagement with this world. After all, I was already maintaining my distance with the world before I took a seat in his class and all he did was provide me with some vocabulary to describe this distance. For that I should always be grateful.

11   Adam Phillips, "Desiring by Myself," *Raritan* 25, no.1 (Summer 2005), 61.

So instead I looked at the books behind his shelf and tried to remember their names. I have to get copies, have to read them fast and well, impress him in the next conversation, I thought. Then I said, yes I will think about it. We fell into a well-made silence, a tailor-made silence like two people holding their breath in competition to find a tiny bookmark misplaced many years ago in a volume of *Jean-Christophe*. As usual, he found it first. He smiled, picked up his lost treasure, his pen, and said, maybe it would do you good to get out there more. Yeah, I said, my roommate said the same thing. He laughed. He said, I mean out of this particular literature. He looked at me. I played with the edge of my sleeve and asked him if he had any suggestions. Hmm you know what, he said, you should really try to go to this symposium or talk or conference thing next week; it's on consumerism and desire. You'd probably enjoy it. Oh where is this conference or symposium or talk thing, I asked. In New York, he said. He said he would send me the details.

A small part of me must have seen this coming. That this was what he would say when I asked him, where. What else could he have said? After all, everything happens in New York. A small part of me already knew it and had been preparing for it. But we could never fully prepare for a sign or test like that. Signs and symbols. Sighs and cymbals. Sitting in the chair opposite his, I felt myself drifting away, sand by sand. I was the sand flowing away in an hourglass. I tried to be light-hearted, still. I said great. I said sure I'll turn myself into a national dish on East 17th Street. He smiled a bit. I was referring to the Instagram post I just showed him, of a plate of colorful nasi lemak against the background of dim Manhattan. The caption was *national dish of Malaysia*. See, all third-world cuisine is doomed to become national dishes, just like all third-world literature is doomed to become national allegories. Put me on a silver plate and I will give you a most problematic exotic encounter. How's that?

I thought about this again when I noticed people drinking Kombucha in the library. Ah, food items outside the Western culinary canon: at once a celebration of inclusiveness and a reiteration of differentiation. Like those foreign porn stars. But this Kombucha, wrapped up in lime green plastic with images of lotuses and dragons, was just an actor faking an accent, happy to be consumed by pretty, loud, pretty loud people in the library. Sometimes you'd think they actually live in that area of the library, eating full meals loudly, whispering loudly, checking their phones loudly, applying make-up loudly, sitting on the table and crossing their legs while chatting with their love interests loudly, flipping through their thick books on introduction to microeconomics loudly, hitting the shoulders of their love interests with their thick books, loudly. They swayed their beautiful heads to and fro. They laughed their beautiful laughs. They drank their beautiful Kombucha. They gossiped about a secret party. They knew very well that a secret party gains its full gravity only when people can hear about it in fragments in a library. There would be generations of such people, including those who, during rush seasons, would be inclined to play innocent pranks on others such as declaring undying love to their back. The people are the river but those long tables near the entrance of the library are the riverbed. The first such people I saw on my first day at school who gave me a weird look when I tried to sit at the same table were not the same people I saw today, who were ostensibly younger and more forgetful.

It was in the library I booked flights and a hotel room. One that was neither too expensive nor too cheap. It was something my mother would do. Standing in front of an aisle in the shop, for instance, my mother would always pick the item whose price was between the two extremes, between shame and guilt. My mother had lips pointing downwards and many people had pointed out that resemblance in me. Perpetually pouting. Anything in me that reminded me of my mother made me a little sad. To distract myself I calculated the distance between where you were and where I would be. Fifteen minutes' walk, give or take. Just enough for two cigarettes. Then I looked up your apartment with Google Maps street view.

Three years ago there was scaffolding all around your building and a French bistro downstairs. One year ago the scaffolding and the French bistro were both gone. I couldn't get a more up-to-date view. I walked around your block virtually to see if there might be an angle of your building from this year, this month, this hour. There wasn't. Instead I had to look at all those shops and restaurants and cleaners and construction sites on that street. The buildings were either gray or red. I didn't know why I found that a bit sad. That the primary colors you saw each day would be gray and red. I wondered if desire has an expiration date. Meanwhile Frankie was sitting next to me eating her Chinese takeout while watching some documentary series called *A Bite of China*. On her screen were the usual images: they squatted, feet deep in soil. They dug up potatoes. One at a time. At first it was all wordless. Then there were those barren conferences, bilateral talks, mines, construction sites, and in the midst of it all a girl was squatting in the soil looking at her own feet and she said, mom, mom I want to study business and find a job, farming is too tiring. Her mom said, but with farming, you will always have work, every day. She said, but it's so tiring. Then she smiled, inexplicably. That whole life seemed so concrete and so ethereal: the land, the oil that keeps dripping into the basin, water bottles and speeches, highest instructions coming out of loudspeakers. Day after day. Followed by images of food. People making a feast out of all this, despite all this, with the camera zooming in on the yellow flour mixed with dirt. Zooming in on their withered hands. Zooming in on steam rushing out of a big clay pot.People eating, wordless again, all smiles. Wall to wall. Face to face. Frankie and I watched them do that while we ate our takeout from a restaurant called Happy China in the library.

As is often the case the Chinese name for that restaurant called Happy China was not Happy China at all but Hong Kong Mansion. I had no idea why all Chinese restaurants like to do that, but they do, assuming an entirely different persona when it's in a different language, like they are too tired to explain to others what they are all about so they just say, oh you know, Happy China. Frankie pointed to her screen and said, remember that old Chinese saying—*to the people, food is heaven*? What we have here is, well, pornography. Why? I asked. Well she said, being oppressed and being obsessed with food always go hand in hand. We are obsessed with food because we have nothing else. Yeah I said, but wait, that's not exactly right. That's not the whole story I don't think. Because you see the genre of pornography was born when sexually explicit artifacts were being locked up during the nineteenth century. It was this gesture of suppression that gave birth to pornography. And in that sense *A Bite of China* probably doesn't qualify because it's sanctioned and even promoted by the state and therefore lacks this subversive element. But, Frankie said, won't you agree we are taught to indulge in food to avoid thinking about the more important things? Even if it's not pornography *per se*, it's a tool for distraction. I began to say, but you see... but was immediately struck by the absurdity of our discussion of mass deceptionwhen the air was rich in garlic and soy sauce. So I just said to her, but you see I don't disagree with you. Frankie shrugged and put her earphones back on. I began to type frantically, with the voice of my advisor echoing in my head, *but, structurally, socially, what could this desire do?* I looked at Frankie who had her eyes fixed on her screen and her mouth half-open. I looked at the other people on this floor, mostly of a different complexion, who were tapping their pens on their books or writing things on their notepads with their eyes too close to the page. I tried to see a so-called community in this image. But no, no, it's no use. Even if we could be said to share the same humiliation, that humiliation is rooted in entirely different traditions and following entirely different trajectories. It's no use. Reality and theory are creatures of two distinct species, refusing to be tamed by each other. And yet we are all guilty of purposefully seeking out new evidence to nourish our preconceived notions. Some would say that's how we lost the election. In a way college had trained us, and continued to train us to do precisely that—so let's come up with an idea and give fodder to it. For instance a thesis of sociality and connection is bound to take shape if we set out to find traces of those things and ignore all signs showing otherwise. To manufacture complexity you could easily drop a footnote saying, oh, but there have always been undercurrents of resistance, let's not forget that. I was so tired of all of it. I was still doing it. I typed in #foodporn once again and looked for captions such as *let's make this; when can we go together?; let's fly to wherever this place is*. I set out to find longing and bonding, invitations and interactions, and there they were. You just need to pay attention and they would be there. Yes, while we do ogle pictures of food on our own, for our eyes alone, we also capture, upload, disseminate, and archive, don't we. And by doing that we are transforming this solitary act into an activity with a social dimension, where the ephemeral object ingested by the body is rendered a subject of material objectification enabling new ways to connect, negotiate, and frame social relations, isn't it? Of course, of course, because

> while the sensual pleasures of eating are completely individualized, eating is still a highly social activity and regulated by the community.

The consumption of food has always been a marker of familiarity and social bonding. Likewise, #foodporn, as a materiality transacted online, constructs a common, permanent visual repertoire that transcends cultural boundaries and affords a long-distance social intimacy. The gaze finds its renewed and prominent place in this cyber-community, where the boundary between the private and the public is blurred through the diffuse practice of "making oneself seen,"[13] of mass exhibitionism, and even panopticism. Yet this community is one built not upon surveillance but rather, a form of familial support and sociality.

The proliferation of digital media and the decrease in cost of production dismantle barriers to enter the arena, where professionals and amateurs alike have their, albeit asymmetrical, share. #Foodporn appeals to an imagined collectivity in taste that obscures class differences, language barriers, and geographical distances. The easy circulation of these photos, which quite literally speak for themselves, provide the ever-expanding opportunity to organize a transnational community.

In the texts narrating #foodporn, the plural pronoun "we" constructs a virtual community. The narrator of #foodporn takes the form of a depersonalized collective voice, echoing

---

12   David, Marshall, "Food as Ritual, Routine or Convention," *Consumption Markets & Culture* 8, no.1 (2005), 71.

13   Luis Dario Salamone, "Objects of Surplus *Jouissance*," in *Scilicet-A Real for the 21st Century* (New Lacanian School of Psychoanalysis, 2014), 225.

the depersonalized individual subject whose forms one finds throughout contemporary literature, of the famous "decentered subject" or "consciousness without the me." It does not mark the death of the subject, however. Instead, this collectivity is a feature common to postmodernity. We have to ask ourselves, then, the important question, "Who is this 'we?'" Who is included in this community? Who is invited to desire?

Two graduate students who were sharing the long table with us were sending us occasional dirty looks, for the smell of garlic and soy sauce, or for being too young, or too loud, I wouldn't know. They were a pair of lovers who expressed their love by rubbing their heads together when one of them was about to head to the bathroom. While typing I got a text from Frankie sitting next to me. She said she overheard the woman call the man *daddy*. No way, I texted back. Way, she texted. I glanced at the piece of paper the lovers had set on the table between their elbows. They were passing that paper back and forth. What could they have written there I wondered. She would write, daddy. And he would write, yes, baby. Daddy, could I, she would write. Or perhaps, daddy, I want to. I was disappointed that even in my perverse imagination everything needs a sign of permission. Then baby got up and headed towards the bathroom. With baby gone, daddy sat there barrenly. He had lost his point of reference and he looked incomplete, like the outline of a drawing. He stared at the piece of paper. As I glanced at him again you sent me a video.

In the video you were in a windy, dark place. I wasn't sure which city it was, but it wasn't New York.

I saw a big billboard. And next to the billboard

you

were holding some equipment I couldn't identify and
you were patrolling the street

with a black beanie on.

It was the first time I saw you and I saw it on video.

Someone was giving cues to you

or you were giving cues to someone I couldn't see.
People

were moving around you in an orchestrated way, like
they were putting on a play

and you were walking in a straight line, looking ahead

showing me only one angle of your face

with half of your face in shadows.

You, ill-lit, ill-defined, and nobody could see

you,

something nobody could see but me.

There was a word in Chinese for this, meaning: *only [I]
have the bright (intelligent) eyes.*

(I must have watched the video at least seventeen
times, and then misplaced it. Or perhaps the video had been
buried in thousands and thousands of pages of text messages,
with my memory being the only proof that it ever existed. For as
I write this now I want to dig up the video and see how I would
feel about it now, now that I know what you look like. But back
then the only thing I felt was that you had a beautiful jawline.
What an image gives is always too modest.)

    In such cases of replacing the camera, and addressing the food
    directly, we become the voyeur again through identification.
    For feminist film theorists, the operation of cinematic
    narrative reinforces psychoanalytic patterns:

the phallus and the language of the father, the positioning of the woman as the other, and the quest for the lack. However, in #foodporn captions, the direct address—acknowledging the presence of the look ("how sexy you look;" "you look so good", etc.)— The texts break down the fourth wall without eliciting discomfort, for transgression is an extolled property in this online community. We are assured that we can indulge in fetishistic thrills, as the captions are shouting "YES" to unofficial, "illegitimate" desires: "I feel weird about how I want this quinoa bake"; "all I need in this life of sins is me and some bagels"; "pancake porn. Sorry not sorry." Whether it is to identify with the food or the camera, we are at ease with our "sins," ever comforted by the acquiescence and even affirmation from the community.

Baby was back, triumphantly, with some banana bread (hopefully not from the bathroom). Baby and daddy broke the bread on our endless desk, in a lavish, absent-minded way typical of lovers. They picked up the crumbs with their fingertips as if their fingertips were magnets. They gathered those crumbs on that piece of paper presumably laden with honeys and daddys and sweet nothings as if they would have the heart to share the crumbs, later, with the less fortunate in love.

I replied to you, tired?

Several hours later you said, tired.

I asked you, wanna say something?

Several minutes later you said, like what.

Anything, I said.

You sent over

a picture in which the billboard had fallen to the ground.

Both daddy and baby had left. Only the piece of paper remained. I picked it up. On it was a drawing of a cat in fine detail, with each hair visible, with its eyes closed. Next to the cat was a triangular thing I couldn't identify. In about two hours' time they had drawn a cat together, stroke by stroke, and exchanged no words. I shifted my gaze back to my screen and tried to write some more. In the back of my mind your video was beckoning me to watch it one more time. Just once, it wouldn't hurt. Indulge me, it said, indulge in me. I asked myself to think about photography instead. Yes, photography, why not. I tried to think whether the body in the picture, your body, is, in some fundamental way, already a lost body, operating only as a trace, like the remnants of a performative love in the shape of a cat. At the heart of photographic representation is an irrevocable sense of loss and cinema, your art, is an apparatus generating lost bodies. Eternal, but lost. Eternally lost. I put my face in my palms and stared at miles and miles of eagerly spreading green outside our window. Frankie was humming a tune next to me. I breathed in the scent of gardenia in her hair. I thought about you again.

But why does it have to be so cold in the room? The air conditioner above my head continued to push out chilled wind onto my scalp that managed to keep me hovering a few centimeters above my seat. That horrible distance again. Or was it really chilled? The sting I felt was like the first few seconds of water I'd get in a hair salon, when I'm still making up my mind about whether the uncomfortable sensation is from the water being too hot or too cold. The entirely white room, so remarkably white I felt I was contaminating it with my presence, was populated by people with audible breaths. Together we heard many things. We heard: *fantasy is always better than reality; the object always already has an imaginary sphere which is fuller.* We heard: *one is nourished by the imaginative dimension. What is at stake in nourishment, in fact, is stupidity.* We heard: *let's allow opportunities for unforeseen bursts of pleasures in a world in which our pleasures are never truly allowed.* The room was very cold and the lights very warm. I looked ahead and saw rows and rows of heads floating above the crimson seats. Heads nodding. Heads nodding off. Heads adorned with objects, a hat on top or a pen behind the ear. The person giving out these words was a man of about forty who looked like he knew a thing or two about little defeats in life, a connoisseur of self-deprecating jokes. Yes, the color of his teeth and his nails confirmed to me that he, too, was a victim of addiction. Yellow; yellowed; yellowing. I jotted down what he said and made it look nice. Yes, you see, this was supposed to be a lecture. But I absorbed it like a poetry reading. That was my problem with theory. I was never there to understand or examine. I was there to be seduced. To be seduced by art, politics, cinema, the symbolic order, the real in the twenty-first century, news, beautiful people, mothers, strangers, beautiful objects, one another. I was all ears and full of ears. For instance I would feel something when they announced that the sexual relationship doesn't exist. I would feel some other thing when later, they announced that women don't exist. I would be at once repelled by and attracted to their brazenness. I hid my phone inside my black leather bag, my wrist bitten by its zip. I texted you. I said, I want to see you.

I looked up again just as a woman in black entered with light refreshments. Whenever light refreshments appear heads move. Heads turn. Heads sway left and right. Bodies would move next. Before bodies begin to move bodies regard one another, evaluating the situation. It was delicious how the undercurrents of desire began to flow in an otherwise purely intellectual room as soon as people saw deviled eggs and mini quiches. Little devils, I thought. Kitsch, I thought. Heads gravitating towards the food while minds were still doing their best to stay where they were. Minds that were soon to be occupied by images of licking and chewing and swallowing while bodies were still chained to the seats. Minds fluttering like kites chained to the seats. The man on stage was saying helplessly one thing after another about meaning and signifiers but the man began to stammer a little, tripping over words. He sounded like he knew he was losing control of the room and I was sorry to hear that. Or maybe he had always been stammering and it was only then we finally saw it.

We were actively looking for this moment of weakness, you see. We had been searching for signs of fatigue or resignation that would give us a reason to stand up and leave the scene. Leave! Quick! A breathing space, if you will. And while the man was being examined we noticed a woman from the corner of our collective eye. A woman in a three-piece suit in emerald green, moving languidly towards the trays. A woman with ridiculously big, sad eyes, and pale, slender muscles, moving as if kite strings were all entangled around her body. We couldn't look away when she picked up a mini quiche and put it into her mouth. She didn't put it on one of those tiny paper plates, even. Who is she? Doing things like that without thinking. She put that thing straight into her mouth and was chewing with supreme concentration and soon afterwards it would be traveling down those dark corridors. Disintegrated, diffuse, flowing down, down, down. We meet at the bottom.

> [Notes on Chapter on What Women Want]
> On the other hand, deliberate choices of food items can be used as an expression less for satisfying sexual instincts than for challenging normalized sexuality.
> Second Sex: girls protest by deliberate acts of perversion and oddities (she eats pencil lead, sealing wax, bits of wood, flies or spiders, sugar soaked in vinegar, white worm found in lettuce— she is attracted to the repulsive.)
> Appetite in literature as a trope for sexuality;
> Religious practices of self-starvation;
> Slender bodies idealized in an apparent attempt to restrain women's sexual desires
> The discourses of maternal domesticity and the concern over body image have always been more prominent and

the pleasure side, the right to rejoice in food consumption, is often downplayed and even suppressed, distancing femininity from food pleasure

The man on stage coughed, drawing our attention back to his throat. *A shared eroticism*, the man was saying. Eroticism being a lonely movement towards the other. The question is, the real question is, whether we could inject a potion of sociality into it. No we couldn't, I thought, no of course not. But the man was promising us so much, too much, you see. I gasped each time he mentioned *new possibilities*. Yes, yes, tell us more. We, people who are cut by language, leaned forward. We listened and wrote. What we wrote down we thought we could add to our own ingredients, home-grown or stolen, to concoct something so miraculous that the steam it emitted brought out tears. A drug to end all drugs. I was writing too. I wrote: *need to read more, and slow down my pace, use the I pronoun more, inhabit those I's.* I wondered what the others were writing at this very moment. I peeked at my neighbor. He was using a real pen, smearing the letters with his shirtsleeves. He was writing, something like: *objects-relation / being, not whole / and why not see a face of the other, the God face?* I couldn't see his face but I wondered whether it would look like mine and I wondered whether what we were doing was sort of an intellectual masturbation in common. I put down my pen and read the text I just got from you. You said, sure.

I said well actually I mean it this time. I'm in New York.

You are in New York, you repeated.

Yes I said, I'm in the same city as you are, if that makes sense.

That must have confused you. I was saying

very simple things and simple things usually confuse you.
You were struck by the same confusion, I'd imagine, as when
a character in a film walks down from the silver screen
and demands attention.
You didn't reply for a while.
In that while the man had finished his talk and we had clapped.
In that while I left the white room and walked several blocks.
In that while I stopped near a tree and lit a cigarette, warming my palm with the flames.
I stared at your name. You were typing.
It felt like hours had passed before you finally said
seven p.m. okay?

I recognized you by your black beanie, the same one you wore in that video you sent me. You walked towards me like you were stepping on invisible insects. Before you were here I was standing in that little square in Astor Place. Some people were spinning dear old Alamo, or rather, *trying to* spin old Alamo, who was especially stoic this day. I appreciated their efforts. When you arrived I could see little particles in the air, dust, or light. You said, hey. You smiled. When you smiled you looked like you were shameless. By that I meant you looked like you had never heard of the word *shame*. You were tall and angular, in dark hues, casting enormous shadows as you approached. You stopped, a few steps in front of me. I think you might have asked me, hey are you disappointed? Why would I be, I said. Because, you said, because things never appear in their true proportions.

You began to speak Shanghainese to apologize for the fact that you might not be the man I was waiting for. When you spoke Shanghainese you looked different. Quick-witted. Provincial. Proud. I had to admit I was a child of migrants and couldn't really speak the dialect. Ah I see, you said. And anyone who speaks it well can easily scare me, I thought. You offered to carry my black leather bag. There was a little hesitation in your voice, like you weren't sure if it was something you'd truly like to do. I caught that hesitation and I said no, no I'm okay. We stood there. Me with my black bag.

You with your black beanie. Someone was again trying to spin Alamo behind us, making pathetic noises. And you smiled again. Perhaps you gave out a chuckle. Several hours later when you kissed me I also gave out a chuckle, in remembrance of yours, as a tribute to yours. I don't know how to move. You'd have to teach me, I thought. We'd have to create a new language on the spot, one that involves the proximity of bodies. But I wasn't able to speak either. I measured one word against another on a scale. The scale flipped over. The things I had been expressing in written words and written words only were muted and when I stood in front of you for the very first time I felt like a skeleton.

I remember other details about those five minutes in disconnected images:

I was putting a book back into my leather bag when you patted me on the shoulder. You said hey. I noticed how that *hey* was coming from very deep in your throat and understood how long you had been saving that *hey*.

Wind was all over my face when I tried to gather my stray hair and secure it behind my ear.

You really are very blonde, you said, you are blonder than I thought. A shortcut I said. A shortcut to what? Well so that I could feel I'm allowed to do anything, and nothing I do would be out of character. It suits your character you said.

I showed you the book. You looked at the cover and said you always wanted to read him.

You were extending a hand towards my black leather bag. No I said. No need. But I might have waited a second before saying that because I kept an image of your hand floating in the air in a suspended way.

This black bag of mine had a knot in its strap and the knot always landed perfectly at my shoulder blade. That made me happy.

Perhaps I had thought about this encounter for too long that when it was finally happening it felt like it had all happened before. Perhaps different things I would observe about you, things that would emerge only some seconds later, some minutes later, some hours later, had crawled backwards past columns of time so that nothing you did surprised me, when you were still doing it.

You hailed a cab, for instance. It was not surprising.
Where to, I said.
Social obligations, you said, have to meet up with some friends. Yes of course I said. I forgot that you could have a life of your own. That you would have other people to talk to, get dinner with, do things with. That you would lend your ear and mind and heart to them, giving them pieces of you. I forgot. That was entirely possible. You took off your beanie in the car and looked through the window most of the time. I looked at you most of the time. The car passed over grids of scenery I would never see, as I was only seeing your fingers resting on your lap, long and agile. You had some purplish stamp on the back of your left hand. I couldn't tell the pattern or the words. Either the stamp had faded or you might have tried to wash it off and then given up. Some trace of it was still there. A vague reminder of where you had been. I had something on my left hand too. A word that kept escaping me, which only came back to me the previous night while I was doing my laundry. I didn't have any paper at the time and was afraid I might lose the word again so I jotted it down on the back of my left hand.

Interpellation, I wrote. *Interpellation*, it read. I was about to take a picture of it and send it to you, but at the same time my laundry was done. I wanted to send it to you after I got back to my room, but my roommate caught me and wanted to discuss boys again. Then I forgot. And now, right now, when you were sitting right next to me in the backseat of a cab, when I finally had the chance to tell you all about it, I realized I couldn't. I wouldn't be able to just give my hand to you. It wouldn't be the same, would it? It would be too in-your-face. Imagine if I intruded into your field of vision with a hand with a strange word on it, and said, hey, look what I've found. The significance of the word no longer warranted the level of justification it required.

When we stopped at a red light you turned to me and asked me how I liked New York.

It's not as I imagined I said, but again nothing is ever as great as I've imagined. Hmm you said.

I said… and you laughed a dry laugh. Then you said it was not something we should talk about. I told you there are no should's in my dictionary. You said you had them in yours. Should do stuff. Should do well.

I was looking at your profile in the night wondering who had seen it earlier that day, in the morning light.

You asked me if I liked what I was writing. Yes of course I said, I have to. I asked what about you. You said you had fallen in love with a troublesome woman. Hmm? Oh, writing, you were talking about writing.

I discovered that you were a scentless being. I smelled nothing. No ambition. No sense of desperation. Not even shampoo or shaving cream or cologne. You were clean and crisp.

You were tapping on your lap. I thought I recognized the song. I saw a loose thread at the edge of your sweater. I wanted to pull it and see what would happen.

The sky outside was a mysterious lead gray like the eyes of a dead pigeon. The news on the radio turned into a weather report. And some woman was telling us that there was a chance it would snow tonight.

Snow in March, can you imagine that?

Yes I certainly can. Everything makes perfect sense.

During a brief silence I wished you would start telling me about your childhood. Grown-ups' books you had secretly read. Broken windows you had looked into. Pears and tangerines and peanuts you had eaten while sitting cross-legged on an enormous bed. Things to which you ascribed no importance. Things I would never know about.

We ended up in a red bar with high ceilings and giant plastic trees where you introduced me to your friends. I noticed your friends were all white and didn't know what to think of it. You pronounced my name. They appeared delighted and it put me in an awkward position. I felt I had to be able to live up to that delight. I sat down next to you leaning on the tinted window. One of your friends was pouring wine for me and asking some questions. For instance where home was. I said Shanghai. They nodded and they passed food along. They didn't ask you or me how we met. Either they already knew or they just didn't care about such things. I buried my face in bowls of food as I began to recognize how uninteresting everything about me was. There was nothing I could bribe your friends with—I couldn't take out that city from my pocket to mesmerize them for instance, it would be too pathetic. And you, sitting next to me, when I said the name of that city you too must have felt confined and defined by our unspeakable hometown. You stretched in your seat like you were shaking off the dust from your past, a past full of beaten smiles and ponderous silences that were stripped off of all meaning. With a glass in your hand you started to talk about a filmmaker I never heard of. All your friends knew him. You were talking technical terms. You threw around one name after another like a football. You caught and held a name in your hands and you laughed a lot. You laughed so much that you had a perpetual half-laugh on your face. They liked you very much, I could tell, and I was for some reason very happy because of it. I was seeing you in your proper milieu I thought, where you were effusive and generous. You must have given them a lot and would continue to do so. While you were talking I tied up my hair, feeling a coldness in my neck as I did that, conscious of how my neck and shoulder must have looked. Your conversation continued to flow and expand. Gazes from the table bounced off from one person to the other like rays of a sunset bouncing in between glass buildings that never fail to temporarily blind me. Tips of your hair were trembling while you spoke. I was dying for a smoke so I put things into my mouth as a substitute. Things I picked up from the nearest bowl. Crunchy and bland. I chewed meticulously while trying to listen to what you were saying. It gradually dawned on me, from your tortuous conversation, that all of you were making some film together. Together together and together together. You mentioned a place. Cleveland, or Denver. It didn't make much difference to me. Nobody asked for my opinion and that suited me very well. I was happy to listen. I was gradually effacing myself, you see, by turning myself into the mouth that chewed, the lips that opened and closed, and the eyes that were eternally unfocused. I gave myself to you and your friends in pieces. You stopped mid-sentence. You turned to me and said, you are aware you are eating popcorn, right? No it can't be I said, I hate popcorn. Yes you do, you said, and you just ate the whole bowl. How did that happen? I asked. A lot of things can happen when you are not watching, you said.

You raised your glass again and again toasting to nothing.

You were even more agitated at this point. You declared to your friends that after three rounds of alcohol everyone is your loyal follower and believer. Oh come on, they said.

Your friends were calling you by your name. They referred to you in third person. It startled me—the ease with which they pronounced that difficult name. You smiled gracefully whenever that sound was made.

You still hadn't talked about your childhood, but I started to see images of you in our city. You were little, so little, wrapped in a coat with little spaceships or little dinosaurs printed all over. You ran through the littered space between stone buildings in your little steps. Collected and cool-headed. Curious and cruel. A little you.

Another drink was drunk. You looked up and saw nothing. You were leaving that little person behind.

When you spoke English you were a different person, with a different trajectory bringing you to where you were today. You were someone who went to Latin boot camps and spent the summer with your great-aunt in some idyllic countryside picking wild berries and singing medieval lullabies.

I wrote your name with one finger onto the wine glass. It was a very nice wine glass. I have no other words for it— it was nice. And it was a nice name. I wrote your name on it, first in Chinese, tracing each stroke with great attention, then in English, all in small letters. In small letters you would appear gentle and kind, how I wished you'd be. You'd appear susceptible to influences. And you were, indeed.

Someone at the table began to play a song he wrote. And you held my hand all of a sudden. I didn't quite understand it. That gesture came from nowhere and seemed to be going nowhere. I didn't even think about whether anyone else saw it. But as I am writing this now I begin to think about it.

I thought again about the fact that you had no scent. That really bothered me. A scentless being was taking hold of my hand and reigning in the room at the same time.

I couldn't admit it to myself yet.

Several hours later we continued to drink at your place and still I was trying to get a scent/sense of you. This time it was just you and me. We were sitting on your floor with our backs against your bed. My spine was curved. I didn't know about yours. You gave me a glass of golden liquid and you spoke of different schools of thought. You spoke of art and poetry and cinema, and methods of reading, and truths and untruths and post-truths, among other cold things. You spoke of languages you always wanted to learn but never started. Then you spoke of how much you drank this week alone and it was really too much. I'd be lying if I claimed I remembered what exactly we talked about. I was making an effort to sound interesting, I guess, and because of that I probably said little. Several months later you would tell me you were feeling the same way. But I didn't know it then. I thought you were probably bored, or tired, or both. During those intermittent silences you would stand up to sit at the windowsill and write in your journal, which you had vowed to never show me. Please, I said, what if I give you something good in return? You were shaking your head. No, no no no no. Some minutes later I went downstairs to smoke. You see a cigarette is not a way to pass or measure time. A cigarette is time itself, all rolled up and fragrant. I smoked up time. I thought about why I had to travel downstairs to do it why not just smoke it on your balcony why not just smoke it in your face. I couldn't pinpoint the exact reason but somehow smoking on your balcony or in your face was not an attractive idea. At this hour at the foot of your building there were still many lost souls, pizza in hand. Walking and waiting. Waiting for something to finally happen to us. You see we never want to take any action but we want everything, everything to happen to us. Many people were smoking too, next to trees and shopfronts, bored in a friendly way. When I returned to you with scents of tobacco and other substances all over my body I was ready to give you everything, everything you never wanted.

(...and as I was waiting at your door I thought of the beginning of a novel I had always wanted to write. The woman lived in the attic of an old building. She was curling up like a cat, perhaps hibernating. In a cold city. Probably Vienna. Or Venice. Or Vilnius. Some city that started with a V, that's for sure. The woman or I—I often get confused whenever I think about a novel I wanted to write because I would automatically think the protagonist is me—was making a grave decision. A decision she had been patiently brewing in her head for hours or days or years on end. One day, she thought to herself, one day I will have the strength to walk down those squeaky stairs and open the front door. It will be snowing outside when I do that. It will be a very cold day that even the snowflakes themselves will be cold to death. I will open that front door, step onto that front porch, and I will say, today I'm ready to fall in love.)

I opened the door to your place and couldn't say a word. When I entered I was surprised to see you, as if I thought youwould evaporate as soon as I was gone. You were still there in full. I looked around to ascertain what else was in this room, like I was seeing it all for the first time. And maybe I was. I saw a bed. A turntable on the floor. A lot of books.

Books on your floor on your windowsill on your desk on your bed. And because they were not placed on shelves, like you would see in a normal person's place, because they were thrown around like that I didn't dare ask about them or pick one up. Precisely because they were left in the open like that they were extremely private. How clever you are.

I threw myself to the floor to be with all your books. Open and private at the same time. Me. You. We drank more and the conversation flowed like honey. You said, tonight we are in Delingha. And I said, sister, tonight I don't care about mankind. I only miss you. What a great poem you said. Yeah, I said. You raised your chin a bit and said you were picturing someone holding a dictionary in his left hand and the dictionary disappeared. Isn't that us, I said. Your eyes rested on me when I wasn't speaking. Mine rested on you when you were. We had a few good laughs, over what I wasn't so sure. I was glad I managed to make you laugh. At the end of one of those laughs we kissed. It was nice. The kiss began to wander. While it wandered I thought about the ultimate limit in the pleasure-seeking activity, and I suspected that you knew it too. That you understood things effortlessly. Of course you would. The essence of things came to you easily. Things I had to read extensively about to make sure of. I wasn't feeling or sensing anything in particular only that you were looking at me in a way that reminded me you were somewhat older.

The night started to flicker. You picked up a guitar. I didn't realize you had one or that you could play. You plucked a few strings.

Through your balcony we could see other scenes from other windows. I was hoping that together we could see a beautiful naked woman and you would say something about her and you would tell me you wished you were in that other room instead of this one and I would say, me too actually.

At some point I wished I wore eyeglasses. So that when you were talking about money, or the lack thereof—a topic I usually pretended I was allergic to—I would use my middle finger to push the bridge down and look at you upwards like I was rolling my eyes.

It occurred to me that in books you don't usually get to know what the protagonists eat for each meal. I guess the assumption is that they have eaten off-stage. And because everything happens off-stage, whether those have been hot hearty meals or flimsy flippant meals is not all that clear. If I were to write a novel I wouldn't do that. I would write about each meal and if there are long periods when no food item has been mentioned you can assume the character hasn't eaten.

You continued to pluck the same few strings. Then you began to tell me a story. Once you were stranded in the middle of the ocean with someone else you said. You didn't know that person well but one thing you knew for certain was that you were in good supply of time on that boat. The idea was that you were stranded in a place where time was unlimited. Together you fought your shadow battles with imaginary figures. You recorded things you wanted to say because you shared a sense of guilt about your past and future, something that had to do with why you boarded this boat in the first place. Days and years passed like that, or they didn't, because you didn't have a real sense of days and years. When you shared your last story together, something about a better future, or a different version of today, you saw a piece of land on the horizon while your companion shot himself up with all the remaining morphine. His pupils dilated. You were both happy in the end.

When our bones were starting to ache from sitting too long on your floor I still didn't know what the moral of the story was. You looked out of your window. Let me show you something you said. You show me mine, and I show you yours I said. You didn't get the joke. Or you thought the joke was too old. You put the whiskey bottle in my hand and you carried the guitar. I followed you onto the balcony where we saw little lights blinking on the horizon, golden veins of the soundless, irreverent city. The city looking like a grand narrative. Some secret code that was never meant for us. In all those lights I felt I, too, was a lightbulb. You motioned towards the balcony of your neighbor's. Nobody lives there you said, and the apartment is so empty it makes good echoes. Right I said. You looked at that other balcony. I noticed a gap in between the two balconies, indicating the possibility of a fall. You must have seen it too. It is no coincidence that the fall of men is accompanied by the emergence of desire, remember? Hey let's climb over you said. Okay let's I said. I must have been really drunk at this point to appreciate how high we were. Your corduroy jacket was full of wind like you were a huge kite that was going to be carried away any minute. I wanted to steal that jacket. Maybe I did, later on. You turned around to give me a smile before you climbed over the railings with your guitar strapped to your back.You stepped onto cement. You climbed more railings. Then you were on the other side. When you were on the other side we looked at each other. You extended your hand to me and I passed you that bottle. Then I followed you over. I had no choice. I followed you as I recited a poem out of order.

Were I like you, or were you like me, I thought. You guess the soul, I thought. We are strangers, I thought. I was on the other side with you.

You slid open the glass door. The large door. L'Âge d'Or. We walked around and I told you that this empty apartment reminded me of an old Taiwanese film, where the characters gathered in all the empty apartments in the city to dance, fuck, celebrate birthdays. Those were some bad years, apparently, with so many empty buildings and so many homeless people. Yeah you said. You said in fact you had met that director once. And the two of you smoked a cigarette together on a balcony overseeing a different foreign city. This happened many years ago. You happened to be in that foreign city for some film festival and bumped into the director in a restaurant. You went over and introduced yourself. You said you were a film student and you admired his work. The director looked at you and asked if you had any cigarettes. You said sure sure I do is this brand okay and as you were saying that and taking your half-empty packet out of your pocket the cigarettes fell to the floor one by one. You bowed at the same time to pick them up. Then you straightened up and he smiled and headed towards the door to the balcony. When you followed him out you promised yourself you'd remember everything the director would say to you but as it turned out the director was stingy with words and the only thing he said to you while smoking his cigarette was, do it well, with a pat on your shoulder. You thought you understood what it meant. I thought I understood what you meant.

We were still walking around. The apartment looked exactly like yours, only empty. It could very well be the place you just moved into, I thought.

So for a second I pretended that it was really the case. That we just moved in here in the middle of a clear and crisp night, with our whiskey and guitar and nothing else. And that we were very happy like that. We came empty-handed and we liked that. You would bring in more books of yours, of course. Boxes and boxes of books. I would be picking at your books and offering useless little commentaries. Stop it you would say. We would share a cigarette before we chop up onions and other vegetables. We would have people over and afterwards you would tell me what you think of them. You would say someone is a poster child of neoliberalism and you couldn't understand how some other very different people could possibly fall in love with each other. It's the biggest mystery in the entire history of this world you would declare. Yes yes true I would say and I would laugh. I would stand in our kitchen and stare at the stove, where something would be simmering and bubbling on top. Perhaps curry. And I would tell you about a dream where I was drowning in curry. You would be walking around the kitchen pretending to be looking for something in the kitchen, while we would both know whatever you might be seeking couldn't possibly be in the kitchen. You would tell me what your dream job is: you would go to other people's houses and read all their books they never have time to read. I would encourage you to apply widely. It might be more important to just apply myself you would say. You would play a song for me and the kitchen would be tiny and steamy. Wait just a few minutes, I would say. I would say please don't move. Please don't change. Just stay exactly where you are. Why is that you would ask. It is very important to me that you don't change I would say.

You'd laugh. You'd laugh at me. I would like to cook a meal for you that you will never eat. It would take ages to cook and we would leave it on the stove or counter and watch it turn cold. You'd be reading something crouching over the dining table and I would stop at the door frame, watching you. What, you would ask. No nothing I just love watching you do things. There would be periods of time when you are not here. I would measure the time when you are not here with coffee spoons and cigarettes. I would think about the lovers you'd already had and you would have and I would feel enriched and reassured somehow knowing that yes you are being seen and you are being loved in all different ways a person can be loved. You would return from shooting something in Cleveland or Denver. It would make no difference to me. It matters only that you are here again, taking up your space in the room. It matters only that I'd be able to hear you breathe again in this room. Sometimes I would think knowing that you exist and that you are doing your things is enough for me. Are you happy I would ask. Tired you would say. But you are happy I would insist. Yes. You would walk over and sit down next to me. A song will be playing in the background. We would both remember the very first time we heard it together and what you said and what I said at the time and how being young we looked at each other as if eternity and time were the same thing.

You smiled. You picked up your guitar and began to play. You played the first few chords several times. Then you sang the song for the very first time:

Lean out your window, golden hair
I heard you singing in the midnight air
My book is closed, I read no more
Watching the fire dance on the floor

I've left my book, I've left my room
For I heard you singing through the gloom
Singing and singing a merry air
Lean out of the window, golden hair

Syd Barrett, you said. James Joyce, I said. Really you said, what have I missed. Syd changed a word you know? Which word was it you asked. Merry, I said, the first merry in the original became midnight. Alright you said. I was feeling small aches deep within, a tiny pain in each bone. What is it I thought. I could feel each single hair of mine turning blue, silently. I felt the process of it turning blue. You playing the guitar. You singing in a voice sealed with alcohol. It was all so beautiful that I wanted to cry and I was becoming really serious about things that I wanted to confess everything and I wanted to tell you many, many lies. You put down your guitar and showed me a video of the song covered by a band in the Netherlands. There was a blue-haired girl who was famously crying her heart out. We were watching her cry in a sea of lights and I didn't know why we got to see this in an apartment that belonged to neither of us in a country that belonged to neither of us, what it was that we were really doing here.

We were both lying on the floor, seeing each other.

You told me a story about you passing out from drinking too much. You woke up in a hospital. Before you woke up what you remembered were scenes with an older you accompanied by music like a faltering cassette. It was nice and scary.

Familiar and eerie. The many years ahead of you. You had lived through it all in the few seconds before you woke up. When you finally did, when you finally woke up, you couldn't really say that what you were experiencing was the reality. You wanted to become a functional human being you decided then, instead of a fictional one.

Does this feel real now I asked you. You looked at something else. I wish you would have said yes, I wish you would have told me that yes this feels like real life.

You told me about the places you used to visit in Shanghai, the rooftops, the bars, the underground scenes. You hadn't been back for many years and it was probably all gone. You asked about my birth year and said oh but you have missed out so much. Tell me about it I said, tell me what it was like.

You began to tell me about it, while your fingers were tracing the shape of my brows, eyelashes, nose bridge, lips, very, very slowly.

What are you doing? I asked.

You said, trying to remember.

We kissed again, this time more deliberate and more ambiguous. I noticed, for the first time, that you had a scar beneath your eye, but I couldn't begin to ask about it.

It's not to say, however, that reality is disappointing; it is that desire is excessive. It is not that we lack things; it is just that there are things that we want.

You took off your jacket and placed it over me.

You said it would be nice if one of us was always broke at any given point (or did you say *broken?*). It would be more fun. That way we could take turns being patient (or did you say *the* patient?).

There was some numbness in my chest. You continued to say things. I was closing my eyes to hear them better.

When I woke up the room was still dark. I remembered the last scene from a dream: I was holding a blood-stained five-euro bill and walking on streets made of knives, feeling as happy as a dying man. Within seconds of waking I realized my unconscious had, as always, grasped something important before my conscious mind did. As soon as I woke up all those organs in my body, long forgotten by their host, were beginning to vie for my attention, as if they were all trying to explain, to start a conversation. I was being introduced to my stomach my lungs my heart my muscles who were apparently fond of violent dance moves. Hello, hello, hey. I collected my bones and sat up. No whiskey, no guitar, no light, no song. I was alone on the eleventh floor with several pains I was still trying to name.

I didn't even think of trying to find you. I just knew you were not there, you were not there hiding in one of those shadows. There was no need to check. Perhaps I had left you behind in my dream, misplaced you in a stack of blood-stained five-euro bills on a street of knives. I walked out of your non-existent neighbor's apartment and closed the door carefully. I was thinking about your other existent neighbors you see. Turning left I stood in front of your apartment, looking at a post-it from FedEx that read *sorry that we missed you*. When I was still doing that, standing, looking, considering, I realized I couldn't breathe. A thousand little drummers were busy messing with my heartbeat.

My heartbeat was everywhere on each inch of my skin but still I couldn't find it. I was drawing in large quantities of air but still there wasn't enough air. I looked at my phone: it was four in the morning.

I walked down your hallway. At this point my entire left chest was a hot mess. My left arm too. It felt like someone decided to make an abstract expressionist painting out of it. While waiting for the elevator I googled heart attack. Although the symptoms were exactly the same: shortness of breath, chest pain, dizziness, nausea. I decided that I couldn't be having one. Otherwise I would have been dead by now. I was still being very logical about it all. For instance when I was standing at your door looking at that FedEx post-it I knew you were not in your own apartment either. I was convinced you were not there not because you had never existed but because you left early for the shoot. Yes it was entirely possible. You didn't have the heart to wake me, yes. I thought you must have walked into the elevator with footsteps as light as rain like I was doing then. Very light until you got to the street. You walked into the rain that would soon become snow, still all very light. You waited in the snow. Then you checked your messages.

Several minutes later you got into a van loaded with all your white friends and all your dark equipment. I got into a cab loaded with the scent of the last customer, the scent of heavy cologne failing to cover up a heavy odor. The cab driver asked me where to. The nearest ER I said. I was having difficulty with words as the pain was growing out teeth, like some little creatures were getting their brand new teeth into whatever substances I stored in my torso trying to eat me up from within. I put my head against the window. I realized I was still wearing your jacket and wondered which one of us looked more worn and faded, me or your jacket. Then I was shivering. It was very cold and snow was falling heavily. I asked the cab driver if he could turn up the heat please. He did it with a grunt but still I was cold. I hid my hands in your long sleeves and pulled up the collar. I couldn't say the jacket smelt like you because you had no smell. It smelt of an emptiness which was in itself meaningful and that almost made me cry. I imagined I would keep the jacket separate from my own clothes and would bury my face into it from time to time to remind myself what emptiness smells like. The cab took a turn. Through the window I saw the Williamsburg Bridge glooming in the mist, haughty and tender at the same time. I tried to imagine what this Bridge had seen over the years, the people who had sighed and fought and watched millions of sunsets at its foot. I'd think of anything to distract myself from the fact that I was having trouble breathing. I thought of you again. I told myself to not think of you. Think of something else. Something useful. I took out my phone and looked at a few more posts hashtagged #foodporn. They were saying to ice-cream, *look at these two cones dipped in Nutella.* They were saying to some pasta, *yes, you look so good, OMG.* They were saying to a cinnamon bun, *this is by far the most beautiful thing we've ever seen.* They were saying to a burger, *1 meat is a solo show, 2 meats is party getting started, 3 meats... now we're talking full blown (get it) mouth orgy!* Suppressing a sudden surge of sickness, I began to type a note on my phone:

[Notes on Jouissance]

Jourir (to orgasm)

Notion of jouissance as the principle that is at once the law and its transgression, a limit built into itself, a nod to the pleasure principle

Does jouissance require an encounter between
bodies?

The possibility of jouissance introducing a short circuit;
the negation of relation to the point of making it
disappear

We are in an era, the age of the simulacrum, where
"semblances of surplus jouissance" are too readily
accessible (Lacan, The Other Side of Psychoanalysis)

The pleasure #foodporn promises also introduces a limit
because the accessibility of the food imagery is always
accompanied by the inaccessibility of the actual food
#foodporn as a "limit experience"

What about the feminine jouissance? That which goes
beyond the phallus and is of the order of the indefinite; a
faint reminder of the post-human

Say it with us: Everything. Bagel. Donuts. For the eater
who wants everything.

Let's say, #foodporn promises a pleasure that transcends
the phallic position, a jouissance without bodies—would
this be something related to feminine jouissance?

Something more, something unspeakable, something
beyond

It suddenly occurred to me that, fuck, I never checked
into my hotel room.

The nearest emergency room was one you would see
in sitcoms from the nineties. Perhaps *Seinfeld*. There would
be one second of an establishing shot of its exterior because
some character injured themselves in a funny way. Funny
because in sitcoms, pain doesn't exist. I walked into the

front door with the self-awareness of a sitcom character and was greeted with the absent-mindedness of a sitcom character. The receptionist asked for my name and date of birth. Then they asked me, on a scale of one to ten, how serious the pain was. I said four. I could definitely have gone higher but whenever asked that question I imagined ten to be childbirth and the old instinct of humility kicked in at my most vulnerable hour. They quickly wrote something down, tied a little piece of plastic around my wrist, and asked me to please wait. So I waited. In the waiting area there was a television. The idea, I think, was to give you something else to think about. Right then the television was showing a true crime series of women-murdered-by-their-lovers-or-lovers-wanna-be. People around me were watching with enormous interest. Supposedly people who also had mal-functioned organs. I took out the only book I had from my black leather bag. I looked at the title and decided that I didn't have time for this. Then I waited. While waiting and struggling to keep various fluids down, I got a message from you. You were having a serious headache you said and you promised yourself that you would never ever write novels in your dreams again. I read the message twice.

I was dozing off on the cold eggshell-shaped seat when they called my name, or some version of my name. I followed the person into a second, smaller waiting area. Here the television was showing sensational images of food. I laughed. The guy waiting in the seat next to mine gave me a strange look. Then he was reading out loud a Wikipedia entry to the woman sitting next to him about how doctors first discovered diabetes. *Diabetic urine, the surgeon Herbert Mayo wrote in 1832, is almost always of a pale straw or greenish color. Its smell is commonly faint and peculiar, sometimes resembling sweet whey or milk.* On television someone was mixing one creamy paste with another, even creamier paste. The audience looked astounded. I felt nauseous again.

The doctor, the only doctor on duty that day who was supposedly responsible for this entire room of desperate people, appeared to be very busy, striding this and that way with an urgent air. When he finally re-discovered me roughly two hours later, I already lost all connection with my chest. So, tell me, he said. I began to explain to him, well, I don't know, it just hurts. I don't have the right word for it. English, I thought, *which can express the thoughts of Hamlet and the tragedy of Lear, has no words for the shiver and the headache. The merest schoolgirl, when she falls in love, has Shakespeare or Keats to speak her mind for her; but let a sufferer try to describe a pain in his head to a doctor and language at once runs dry.* That's Virginia Woolf. And then Susan Sontag also said some lovely things about how pain in others always comes with doubt. But of course the doctor didn't have time for it. He nodded repeatedly to himself and he said he would do an ECG for me. Great I said, without knowing what's so great about an ECG. All acronyms terrified me but I need to have a little faith in others.

I was directed to a bed where I was asked to strip. They stuck many mischievous-looking little things to my body. They kindly asked me to please wait. So I waited. I was still making an effort to breathe. And whenever I succeeded it hurt. Everything hurt. All air was being squeezed out of my chest and I thought I was screaming but in fact I didn't make a sound. I was very nice and quiet about it. I thought of you again. I couldn't help it. A few hours ago you told me you were having a terrible headache. And I didn't respond yet. I thought you would fall into pieces if I didn't respond, or responded only many hours later. You would be standing next to some fluorescent lights staring at your phone falling into pieces. You must be. Otherwise why was I falling into pieces here on this cold bed? It only made sense. Thinking about this I tried to sit up and get my phone but got distracted by those beeping signals. Then a nurse rushed in and asked me to please lie down again.

Medical professionals talk in proclamations. It feels like they are talking in order to shut you up. After the ECG, the doctor glanced at the results and proclaimed, you don't have any heart issues. After taking several tubes of my blood the nurse proclaimed, you have anemia. Okay, I said. Is that why no one wants my blood? Putting your jacket back on I continued to tremble. The doctor took another quick look at those papers with figures and graphs showing how my organs were doing. Then he looked at me. His eyes were blue. I looked into his eyes and got a little scared because they were way too blue, blue beyond blue. I felt I could almost swim in them, or better still, drown in them. Hey would you seduce your patient I thought. Then I got distracted by thoughts about food. I hadn't eaten in a while and what I was feeling then was a mixture of hunger and nausea. I looked at him and I no longer saw a person. I looked around and didn't see people. I saw skin, hair, blood vessels, tongue, lips, and bones. My mind was full of scissors. The doctor looked at me with his blue eyes and he said, we don't know what you have. My guess is that it's gastroesophageal reflux disease. And what is that I asked. He repeated the term, and then added, also called an acid reflux. What can you do to fix it I asked. Well I'll give you some pills that you can take he said, but most importantly you have to watch what you eat. What can I not eat I asked. He said, well, alcohol, nicotine, caffeine, carbonated drinks, chocolate, lemons, oranges, tangerines, in fact all citrus fruits and juices, grapefruit, pineapple, tomatoes and tomato sauce and naturally, pizza. He paused. I said is that all? He said oh and also dairy, nuts, all desserts, fried food, spicy food, fatty food, raw food, onion, mint and mint flavored things like chewing gum. That's a lot I said. Yeah unfortunately, he said.

When Frankie learned about what happened she said, we probably shouldn't have starved ourselves that often. Probably not I agreed. I was screwing open my little orange bottle. Does this thing really help Frankie asked. Yeah I'm doing better now I said. I swallowed a tiny pill with some water and it got stuck in my esophagus like an olive. I had been having trouble swallowing, which was something new, and every little something that was new was very exciting, as it attested to the complexity of the issue. The numbness was still there, though. But at this point I was so used to it that it felt like something given, a little feature of living in fact. In fact my first memory of being alive was the memory of being nauseous and dizzy and always tired, of throwing up a lot and crying because I felt dirty. Well this sounds dramatic, so I should probably mention I have nice memories too. I remember I was drawing little flowers and princesses with crayons on the white bed sheets in a hospital. I could have been drawing these things for months, or years, I had no clue. Time loses its relevance when you are drawing, or sick, or very little. My mother was sitting by my side on the bed and she was explaining to me that what I had was something called typhoid. Typhoid I said. The word in Chinese is almost lyrical, combining the character of *hurt* and the character of *coldness*. A hurtful coldness. A cold wound. I was drawing and talking about wanting to become a painter. That's wonderful my mother said, why not. I remember the nurses' eyes, indulgent and apologetic. Why did they never ask me to stop drawing those childish things onto the white sheets? I wondered. I had so many questions about the grown-ups. But I never questioned the pain. I accepted it wholeheartedly. I must have thought this was what being alive felt like. What I didn't know was that a child's gullibility is sincere and diminishes day by day. You know what you should do, Frankie said, you should try this acupuncture place. It really works. Frankie pulled up an Instagram page with pages and pages of pictures of women in pastel pink overalls all stretched out looking very relaxed. Yeah I said, but I'm afraid of needles too. Frankie shook her head slowly.

While Frankie was shaking her head you were texting me, the same topics, alcohol, headaches, books, your dreams, the moon. You finished the shoot and words started to flow again. You made it seem like nothing had changed. You asked me if I had left. Left where I asked. The city you said. Well of course I said, I have other things to do. I was back with my library and my books and on this particular day when you asked me if I had left I was reading an obscure French novel in which an obscure French man was saying these words: *That is to say…nothing. Yes. I have time, a long time. Who has left? You. You alone.* It was then I suddenly remembered a conversation we had when we were on your floor. You had said, it would be very nice if all novels only had beginnings and endings. Then it'd be poetry I said. You paused, like you were thinking about it, and you said, poetry. Good one. I like that. I realized I thought about you less often these days. I thought about you only when I encountered a shadow of you in my readings, like now. I was still wearing your jacket. I was still feeling cold. Frankie took off her earphones and said hey

I'm watching this movie that's super weird. You might enjoy it. I peeked at her screen and saw a pair of lovers passing a raw egg yolk from one mouth to the other. This is really way too much Frankie said, I thought I was watching a movie that will teach me how to make ramen. Just as Frankie was saying that, the egg yolk broke in one lover's mouth, finally. Liquid yolk, liquid golden yolk, tightly contained by a semi-transparent membrane until the tip of the teeth pierced through, flowed down from the corner of her mouth. She closed her eyes and trembled in what could only be an orgasm.

> Sex pornography presupposes that sexuality—the path to gratification—is centered around the phallus: the staging of the phallus drives the plot, and the plot almost always culminates and consummates with male orgasm. The representation of female pleasure poses as huge a problem for pornography producers as for psychoanalysis. Even when a woman is shown claiming, "I'm coming," how do we know she is not faking it? Kulick explains that there are two solutions, either by ignoring it (pre-1970s stag films, for example, were indifferent to women's orgasm) or else by portraying a woman's invisible pleasure by showing close-ups of a man's visible ejaculation.[14] Pornography as a genre is continuously haunted by the impossibility of depicting female pleasure.

> #Foodporn, on the other hand, allows us to revel in a fantasy independent of sexualized human figures. Let us be reminded that when Freud claims that girls reproach their mothers not only for not giving them a penis,

---

14   Don Kulick, "Porn," 80

but also for not giving them enough milk,[15] he is positioning milk/food as the equivalent of a penis in terms of the sexual pleasure it could afford. A similar substitution is happening in #foodporn, where the visual power of the phallus is usurped by food. Food as the central figure abolishes the presence of the body of the other in a traditional sexual encounter. It provides a shortcut to pleasure—the negation of relations between bodies, and in particular, the denial of the phallus.

Half an hour later, I was walking towards my advisor's office with these fresh pages. On my way from the bus stop to his building it began to drizzle. The sort of drizzle that made you feel like you were a plant being misted. I didn't take the time to tell you the weather here changed. Usually I would tell you. Suddenly I wasn't so sure why I would do that. I wasn't sure, either, what to say to my advisor. I didn't prepare any questions and when I arrived at his office I was terrified to realize that in fact I didn't *have* any questions. My head was entirely empty. Not a single thought. Nothing. Whenever I felt like that I felt I had sinned. I probably thought my job there was to have questions. In a moment of panic I would burst out ridiculous things somewhat related to the human condition, or my misunderstanding thereof. On this particular day, I was going on and on about the lack of foundation, and then I digressed. I said, so, sometimes I feel that all I have is just empty time that I'm filling up with words.And I'm fairly certain that there's some misunderstanding between us precisely because we are using the same words. For instance my blue pencil is not your blue pencil. It's not the same pencil. We refer to it as a pencil nonetheless for lack of a better word. He nodded. Are you disappointed by something?

He asked. I couldn't really answer that. He was playing with that ambiguous pencil on his desk. Then he said, you shouldn't feel obligated to explain away your feelings. I'm not trying to I said. I realized I sounded like I was arguing with him over the essence of some petty emotion of mine, and that really wasn't my intention. Luckily he, like all professors, had the generosity to disregard the accidentally personal and meet you where the air is colder and the world is fainter. He sighed, paused, and said, well at times you might feel that you won't be able to translate yourself, but that's precisely why we are doing this; we are trying. Yes of course I said, I know what you mean.

When I shut his office door behind me I stood there enfolding my fingers into a fist and unfolding them again. I did that several times. Then I began to walk down the hallway. I regretted what I said. I regretted what I did not say, could not say. Why am I always equivocating I thought. I was walking without any purpose. It was raining heavily all of a sudden—I found that out when I realized I couldn't produce a credible fire with my lighter. I tried several times and gave up.

April began and I couldn't sleep. Or rather, I never knew when I was asleep and when I was awake. There were no clear boundaries between the two states of being. I drank more. I put more glasses down. I no longer knew when I began to do any of these things or when I eventually stopped. One of those nights when I was in Frankie's apartment I crawled into her bathtub and dyed my hair blue. I couldn't remember the reason. I do remember spending half an hour scrubbing her bathtub to get rid of stains of hair dye, while Frankie was in her living room furiously typing away. But I was so happy doing that, kneeling in her bathtub, scrubbing. I imagined I must have looked like a B-movie character with very little self-knowledge. Around this time I also developed an impulse to grab things. At parties I lay my hands on stray objects and weighed, pressed, squeezed them. I couldn't let go. Once I was holding a pepper shaker the entire time I was talking to someone, perhaps two minutes, perhaps two hours. And the entire time he was trying to pretend he didn't see it. I wish he could have asked me, simply, hey what's with the pepper shaker. But no, he never did. Instead he was very keen to talk about monopoly and how that's very bad. What a shame. Otherwise I would have told him it was a pepper shaker made of good wood and worth fondling you see. I wish I were someone from a nineteenth-century novel who would walk into a room and immediately know what kind of wood the desk was made of. I wore your jacket everywhere.

Nobody knew it was yours, not even Frankie. We were sitting in the school's smallest theater and she said, this jacket looks old. Why haven't I seen it before? Maybe because it's too old I said. It didn't make much sense but she let it go. Frankie was scrolling on her phone and casually recommending another product to me, a juice that will supposedly knock you out within thirty minutes. From Instagram again? Yeah she said, but it really works! Besides they come in beautiful glass bottles with your name printed on them. So, prescription juice, I said. We all want to feel very special don't we. The sun must have come out just for me. Your words that keep popping up on my screen must be just for me. This show is better put on just for me. The show was supposed to be a modern take on Samuel Beckett's *Endgame*. How do you do a modern take on the last modernist I had no clue. Oh people use words loosely these days, you said, unlike you. Not everyone is you, you said. Too bad I said, but also very good. Did all that rhyme with *drool*? I turned right and looked at Frankie who wasn't really looking at me and was texting another friend of hers. Frankie had other friends. I always forgot. I had other friends too, and I sometimes forgot. It's always convenient to forget about such things and unsettling to remember them again.

When I was still trying to get Frankie's attention by looking at her in a slightly inappropriate way I saw something. Fragments only. Some knuckles. The curves of some arm. Blue shirt sleeves rolled up to some elbows. Then I felt the temperature of some eyes before I even saw them. I unfocused my gaze and shifted it back to Frankie entirely, who was finally raining her attention on me. We like that, don't we. We like it when we know others are looking at us but we are not meeting that gaze; we like feeling entirely effete and eternally external to the looking.

There should be a word for the state of being at once conscious and neglectful of the look when something mellow is flowing within us as if our blood were being warmed up like saké. Look, everything was splendid and mysterious, such as Frankie's face. There were things she didn't like about her face but it was almost moving to see its moves. She must have been speaking to me for a while now, because finally I heard her say, hey, I think they are about to start.

For the first several minutes when some guy on stage was still busy stepping onto a ladder or opening up a lid of a trash can I was thinking about whether the slight pop, pop, popping in my veins was connected to my heart beats because if so my heart beats were really too fast. Frankie was negotiating her weight with her seat, making a hissing sound as the fabric of her dress greeted the plastic chair. The dress was a gift. On one of those first spring days when it was still way too cold to wear a dress, she told me where it came from. A little town where she spent her winter break going from place to place interviewing people who had seen true suffering but didn't know what it was, who had no other option but to reconstruct their memories. So how did the interviews go I asked. She couldn't bring herself to tell me about it. She always brushed it off. I resorted to imagining old clocks that would never tell you the right time, tea leaves floating around the edge of a porcelain cup, her shifty eyes landing on various objects in the room like dragonflies. There must have been a sorrow so deep in those interviews that she couldn't even begin to tell me what was said. Instead she talked about the watermelon-colored dress, and a guy. A winter when she had very few cigarettes and during a break from those interviews she was standing in front of a shop window smoking one of her last.

The guy was with her. They looked at the dress together, wordlessly, until she finished her cigarette and left the scene. But whether, while she was still looking at the dress, she was thinking about a distance so enormous between her and this town that even if she wanted to comment on it she would find no words, absolutely no words, or, about how a corner of the world was cracked open and great water the color of primrose was beginning to flood in, I had no clue. Frankie only told me about the few short minutes when she was mesmerized by the dress, and about the guy who would, eventually, buy it for her. The dress was the only thing she could talk about, just like the apple strudel. I could very well be imagining all this.

The guy on stage laughed. I tried to think about what I ate that day. A spinach scone in the morning, no doubt, with too much butter perhaps. No coffee, I don't think so. But what did I have for lunch? The guy on stage lifted a white sheet to reveal another guy. In the light. In a blue shirt and a purple robe. With a red handkerchief covering his face. His chin was raised. And yes, he was the ensemble of the fragments I saw earlier. Then he removed the handkerchief covering his face. And the feeling of suffocation I felt—we felt—in that second was almost spiritual. I had seen him before, yes. Or heard him before. Or perhaps I hadn't. The trouble was, he was good-looking, and good-looking people always make you feel like you've seen them before. They had a way with you and could have their way with you with their easy familiarity. So there he was, this familiar stranger, sitting motionless in a lone chair without eyes. I meant him, not the chair. I mean yes the chair didn't have eyes either, but that's not the point. The point seemed to be that he was blindfolded. So the modern take, as it turned out, was that the Hamm character was not blind but merely blindfolded. That is all fine with me. But after another while he began to say things. He began to say, *can there be misery loftier than mine?* I could feel people smiling knowingly in the dark. He was way too young to be doing that without thinking. He had to think. His beautiful eyes—I was sure they were beautiful—were visibly moving underneath the blindfold. And because he had to think the whole thing wasn't very convincing. Difficult role, I thought. A paralyzed king. He looked as if he were paralyzed by his beauty and that was again, fine with me, with everyone I dare say, because he was great fun to look at. At this point my left arm was numb as I felt what could be my heart beats extending to my limbs, my neck and then everywhere. Just then, he cast a glance in my direction. In that glance I again felt I had seen him before. But where? From a party, perhaps. Perhaps he was the person I saw from across the room. As he continued to look this way I became almost convinced that it was him. It was certainly him. I was losing connection with everything apart from this conviction. I turned to Frankie as if I were trying to confirm my hypothesis, but her eyes were fixed on the stage, her lips glistening. I was alone and safe with my conviction. He began to say on stage, *it's time it ended and yet I hesitate to—to end.* I glanced at the brochure and read his profile below his picture. A first-year. I spelled his name several times. As if the name could provide some clue to a puzzle I hadn't yet been given. I tried to move my shoulders. But how alien it was. Everything was. The shoulder. The arm. The hand that was holding the brochure. At once mine and not mine. Later on when I began to explain to the doctor again I would say, no not really pain. I mean it is painful, sure. But what's scarier is not the pain but the fact that I couldn't feel it.

And how long has this been going on, the doctor asked me. Oh a very long time, I said, my mother in her twenties couldn't get out of bed for days. You mean it's hereditary he said. No no not really, I said, I mean it's been going on for a long time, years, like I said. The doctor started to read some files on his computer screen. A few minutes later, he asked me what the most recent symptoms were. I counted them again, the numbness, the sickness, the throbbing sensation like my heart was sending electrical signals down the veins. But your heart is fine he said. Yes I nodded, that's what I've been told. He then asked about my eating. I told him that although I had bad eating habits I didn't have an eating disorder. He looked at me. I said, trust me, I know this. I'm writing a thesis on food porn. And what is that he asked. The pornographic treatment of food I said. He didn't look too reassured. After some routine checkups he suggested that we do an endoscopy to find out what was wrong. Would it hurt I asked. You would go completely under he said, don't worry. That's great I said, I don't want to feel anything anymore. Immediately after I said that I was a little annoyed with myself for being so theatrical with a doctor. But the doctor should already be very used to theatrics. He tried to smile at me. He asked me to fill out some forms and observed me write. I wrote each word very carefully like I was writing an exam.

The doctor then asked me to please wait and stormed out

of the room. Left alone I began to google is *endoscopy painful.* There is apparently a new thing you could do: You can swallow a capsule with a tiny camera placed inside. The capsule-camera will travel through your digestive system, take pictures, get acquainted with your organs, participate in the digestive process, and finally flush down the toilet. *Don't worry, you won't need to retrieve the capsule.* Euphemism for *don't worry, you won't have to stick your fingers into your own shit.* How nice.

When the anesthetist came into the room I studied him and thought he must have an unsentimental view of things, an insider's view. The anesthetist was young and eager to know everything. He asked me how many cigarettes I smoked every day. I said I quit. He then asked me how many sexual partners I had, and I said none. I didn't know why I lied on both counts.

I was heading out, when the anesthetist said, by the way, you need to get someone to pick you up after the procedure. That's not necessary I said, I can manage. It's not that, he said, it's our policy—it's required. Oh, okay, I said. I put various papers into my bag and nodded.

After I left the room I fished out my phone and began to compose a message to you.

I began to type, so it looks like...but then, while I was still thinking about what to say

I saw that you were typing. I stared at the three little dots and waited. I didn't know what I was expecting.

The school hospital had very long corridors, with color-coded doors leading towards

different exits.

I was getting lost in the various colors while you were still typing. I laughed

at myself because I could never imagine you walking
through these colorful doors, in fact, even if you were here
even if you were here you wouldn't be here to pick me
up I'm sure.

You wouldn't be able to find me.

And you were still typing

typing, typing, typing

and finally what I received was

oh, but what do I want? Secrets—boring, abstract secrets.

(Meanwhile I was walking through yet another green door
opening up to another corridor and seeing your message
I wanted to throw away my phone immediately but there was not
one single window

open. I tried several. Not one open. I gave up.)

What do you mean, I replied. What secrets. I don't
understand.

Secrets, you said, hidden history

an unopened world. Unpredictable. New possibilities.

Otherwise, everything would rot.

If Sisyphus didn't roll the boulder, he'd get fat.

Perhaps secrets are in math, or puzzles, or poetry.

If the poet's Aurelia never married I wonder

if the poet would still fall in love with her.

But the poet would probably live a long life.

you see I'm just feeling guilty that I live on an island and
cannot share life with others.

(When I finished reading your long monologue I was
back to the beginning. The original green door

or perhaps it was a different green door. I sat down on the
floor.

I wanted to get out, and smoke, and cry, if I could.)

I sat on the floor and you were still typing typing typing. More things reached me. Quotes in different languages from books on your floor, journals and diaries of dead people, news articles, book reviews, social media, conversations with others, sightings of strange things flying by your window. Holding that pile of words in my hand I was slightly confused. You confused me. More than the fact that I couldn't get out, that there was no exit in sight in an institution that's supposed to make you feel safe you confused me. But how could you not recognize me. How could you not recognize me, alone on this floor. How could you not recognize me. I didn't know why I was so disappointed to find out what I knew all along. Then I thought:

The ego is first and foremost a bodily ego.

I might have drifted away for a bit on the floor. I wasn't sure. I only realized I had been drifting away when I got an urgent call from Frankie. Where are you she asked. At the hospital I said. Funny that there are exit signs everywhere but not a single, actual exit I said. I will find it soon I promise I said. I was getting up from the floor as I spoke. Frankie sounded worried, perhaps even a little upset, and she was asking me all sorts of questions like why I didn't tell her I was going to the hospital how could she not know how was I feeling. Sometimes Frankie accused me of keeping things to myself, like now. She would say that I have this habit of saying things, important things, in a way suggesting that they are just a footnote, and it's only because she knows me so well that she can see and care about what's important to me. Yes yes I'm aware I said and I'm sorry I'm like that. But really I just didn't want to worry her. Frankie was still speaking. I could hear the sound of upbeat music and muffled talk, everyone being very breezy and sweet towards one another. She must be at Wholefoods. Yeah Frankie said. She told me that she was buying me an oatmeal and would hand-deliver soon. I laughed. I was looking out of the window. Some birds with a bit of blue in their feathers were resting on the branches and putting their heads under their wings. Tiny things like these. And she was right that she would probably never know about them. Tiny things like hearing her voice describing to me what was on the aisle at Wholefoods while looking at some pretty unnamed birds cleaning themselves.

And how long has this been going on Frankie asked. Oh longer than I care to admit, I wanted to say, but it would sound hyperbolic wouldn't it. So I just shrugged. She hugged me. It was nice. I was opening my mouth. I wanted to tell her all about it but after the first three syllables I stopped speaking. If I speak, words and phrases would become you, replace you, to the extent you were not already replaced by them. Frankie was patting me on my back as she continued to hug me. I felt I should probably whimper a little in a situation like this but I wasn't able to. In the end I just said to her that I was a bit tired and wanted to focus on this pain I had, which was real, or so I thought. I said I want to pet this pain and feed it, well not feed it, maybe, at least not quite literally. Frankie shook her head that was resting on my shoulder and said, you know what your problem is? Your problem is that you take metaphors literally.

This happened when we were sitting with our legs crossed on an outdoor table between the two libraries where international students habitually gathered to smoke. We let our cigarette butts stand on the table like little soldiers. Little soldiers against a leap of leopards that were Frankie's canvas shoes. I still hadn't told her about the endoscopy. I knew she had back-to-back classes that day. If I told her she would feel obliged to skip them. Instead I told her about the writing. I said to her, so I've decided that nothing is important apart from the writing. You see, it's the only thing

I have left. Oh don't be dramatic Frankie said, it's just a guy. Yeah, I said, it's just a guy. We let the phrase linger. Sometimes there is a magic in the repetition of a phrase that convinces us of its truth. It all starts with a lack, I wrote in my thesis. It all starts with a lack. It all starts with a lack. Frankie took out several pages of her own draft and started to read something to me. She had a masterful opening, almost as good as *Most people feel guilty about masturbation.* I wish I had something like that, instead of *What is sexy about food porn?* She went on to quote those old Chinese sayings we all know by heart: *Filial piety is the most important of all virtues; There is no filial son for a chronically ill parent; The Master said, while his parents are alive, the son may not go abroad to a distance. If he does go abroad, he must have a fixed place to which he goes.* The decline of that moral discourse. The rise of the utilitarian individualistic paradigm. The end product of a social vacuum. We had been working on very different models indeed. I was quoting people who wanted to kill the Father while she was quoting people who wanted to redeem the Father.

When she finished reading she placed those few pages under her feet; it was windy. She didn't say another word. I couldn't tell if she was sad or just contemplative. I looked at her profile in the sun, and for a while this image trembled a bit in my vision. Soon I won't be seeing her every day, I thought. Soon we will be going to different places. Neither of us knew where we were going but somehow we knew it wouldn't be the same place, not even the same country. And we both knew how difficult it is to move from one country to another, to speak differently, to maintain a different posture, to wear a see-through shirt for the first time. Frankie blinked several times in the sun. She said she was tired of speaking and would like to listen to some music for five minutes,

is that okay. Of course I said, why would you need my permission?
I don't know she said, just thought it'd be polite. Don't mind me
I said, I have a rich inner world and can entertain myself. Frankie
put on her earphones and continued to reply to new messages. I
glanced at the name—I didn't know him. I looked away.

People were passing by our table while eating all kinds
of things on the go. Sandwiches. Muffins. Crepes. Even bowls
of curry that looked like shit. I once had a dream where I was
drowning in curry only to find out that it was actually shit. A girl
walking by caught my eye for a split second. Unfortunately I cast
a glance in her direction just as she was taking a bite into a burger.
And cheese, or mustard, or I don't know what, exploded from the
corner of her mouth. Most unfortunate, and she acknowledged it
with an apologetic (or mischievous?) smile. Please, please, please
stop thinking about shit, I said to myself.

I began to write on the back of a page from Frankie's
thesis:

sexualization of calorific pleasures
        the indulgence in calories is something perverse,
something to be ashamed of
Is it disgust, or is it shame.
Is it shame, or is it the inhibition of pleasure.
Yes we feel shameful about the shit we make. Yes we feel
shameful about the extravagant food we crave. So we say,
this is kinda gross not gonna lie, sorry. So we refuse. And the
gesture of refusal—while still eating, like she was doing, and
still watching, like I was doing—reveals the attachment to a
fetishistic pleasure that we refuse to abandon.
look up how many times the words "guilty" and "ashamed"
are used in these posts

Frankie was still listening to her music. I looked up from my page and saw someone walking towards us. His steps were slow. Fragments of a youth. Muscles and skin. It was a day with a brilliant sun out. As soon as I caught his eyes I had to look away, because it was all too bright. In the next two seconds I quickly checked my bag even though there was nothing in there that required my immediate attention. Then I lit another cigarette. I'd always light a cigarette whenever I wasn't sure what to do at a given moment. But I knew, when I was pretending to look at other things, that if I ever turned to him again the look would still be there, waiting for me to meet it, as if he were promising that he would never look away. Frankie was right, I was guilty of giving things unrealistic meanings. Let's just keep it simple, I thought, he is looking at me. But sight is a genteel sense, some theorist once said. We must first recognize that seeing is a distinct source of pleasure, some other theorist once said. I see things, but things look at me. Baudelaire's subject is smoked by his pipe. As he continued to look at me I felt like I was the pipe seeing and consuming him. He was getting closer. One step. Two steps. Still all very slowly. Slowness in a person's movements always invites trust, doesn't it? His steps had taken him to our table now. There was still time to let him go. If I looked down at my page at this moment it would all be over. *It's time it ended and yet I hesitate to—to end.* I looked up again. He was still there, only a few paces away from us. I raised my chin. I said hey. He stopped. When he stopped and finally looked at me in a more immediate way he was eclipsing. By that I mean he reminded me of the moment when the sun is tamed and everyone is on their balcony waiting for it to be captured, captured by shadows, captured by millions of cameras. Such a grand and beautiful thing, eaten. I jumped off the table. I walked towards him. I still had that cigarette between my lips. It felt good walking towards him with my blue hair and my cigarette. I was in front of him. And my first thought, when I saw how he raised one corner of his mouth to indicate his attempt at a smile, was that I could never love him. But why? I could never love him, I thought again with more conviction. Hey, may I ask you a question I said. He said sure. He didn't ask me who I was, which was telling. But it was surprising that he had a very little voice in real life, unlike that voice he used on stage. Almost inaudible. I had to pay attention to catch it. I wondered how many different voices he could easily pull off. And I said to him I know it's a bit weird but if you have time tomorrow afternoon would you like to pick me up at the hospital. Oh what happened he asked. He seemed concerned, but also strangely delighted. A delight I often detect in men whenever I hint that there's something slightly wrong with me. Nothing serious I said, just a checkup, but would you? Okay sure he said, sure what time?

I walked back to Frankie with a feeling bordering on triumph. When I looked back at the messages I sent to you that day I noticed I had adopted a more flippant tone. I climbed up the table again and leaned against Frankie's shoulder. Frankie took off her earphones and asked, what was that? Oh nothing, I said. She said, well. Yeah I said. Meanwhile I watched him walk away, carrying his backpack on one shoulder, down the stairs leading towards the engineering building, where the cafeteria served pita wraps that tasted like plastic.I thought about the eclipse again. The last few seconds of it. In that split second when the moon is reluctantly departing, the sun has a strange rosy color, like it has blushed because of the touch, the touch of shadows.

And when that touch ends, the moon is still the moon. The sun is still the sun. But I'm no longer the me six minutes ago. I was about to say something to Frankie when I felt another rush of liquids coming up my throat. So suddenly that I couldn't even open my mouth. I couldn't even speak. I forgot I was a speaking being. I felt mocked. Frankie lifted her eyes from her phone and asked me if I was okay. I swallowed. I said yes.

In my latest draft I had written *breath* instead of *breast* and my advisor circled it out and wrote *Freudian slip?.* In the mirror, half of my left breath was showing underneath the badly tied blue robe made of paper—there was no way I could tie it without exposing myself somehow. For some perverse reason, this cupboard-sized changing room could only be opened from the outside—I had to wait again, with my breaths dangling. Breaths, a symbol of the prototypical sexual desires. Yes, pleasure does start from the mouth doesn't it. Our first experience of pleasure is sucking at our mother's breaths. Since nothing is ever forgotten, the memory of breath-feeding continues to serve as the primordial form of pleasure. Freud calls it a *cannibalistic pregenital sexual organization*, ha ha. What he meant is that breath-feeding was a golden era when sexual activity has not yet been separated from the ingestion of food. That's why when we talk about a sexual hunger, or a sexual appetite, we are calling upon more than convenient metaphors. The door finally opened. The young nurse looked in and asked me, ready to go? Sure I said. I was led into a bigger room and asked to lie down on a bed. There I thought about my mother. My mother who couldn't get out of bed for days when she was in her twenties. My mother. My mother once told me that the endoscopy was the most painful thing she ever had to endure. More so than childbirth? Definitely she said, a lot more. I didn't believe her.

Her eyes were soft and noncommittal as she stirred her coffee. More painful than childbirth? Must be a lie, I decided. Must be part of her agenda of making me eat well and reproduce. But again she did all her endoscopy sessions fully awake in the nineties. All her life she did everything fully awake so that later on I could afford dreaming. I was staring at the fleurs-de-lis patterns on the ceiling. Why were there fleurs-de-lis patterns on the ceiling? Meanwhile, robed people were picking up one thing and putting it down again next to me giving out metallic sounds. I couldn't bring myself to look at what they were doing. Their gloved fingers were hovering above my face and I thought about your fingers. I wondered which fingers were more tender. A tube was put into my mouth. Breathe, a voice said.

Breathe, I did. I inhaled. When I exhaled, I felt blisters in my mouth and my jaw was completely numb. I saw massive, quiet blue, and vigilant, inquisitive white. The sounds of metals kissing. Robed people with masked faces and gloved hands, still picking up one thing after another and putting it back down. Nothing seemed to have changed but then a voice said, ah you are awake. A voice with a special effect, like it was coming from a place far away or a place deep within. I blinked several times. Then the voice said it's okay it's all finished. So the difference between being anesthetized and being asleep, I discovered, is that when you wake from natural sleep you still have a vague sense of the passage of time. Yes, you'd feel that some amount of time has indeed passed. But when you are anesthetized, time is confiscated, like a jump cut in a film. You pass from one second to the next assuming it's the same for everyone else until someone tells you that no no, many things have already happened, we've all been through it, it's only you who are many hours behind.

There was cloud or fog or smog in my head as I tried to think. I couldn't think. I was only aware of the fact that there seemed to be drool around the corner of my mouth and I was ashamed. I wanted to raise a hand to wipe it off but my hand was not yet entirely mine. I closed my eyes. A hunger was brewing inside of me like a thunderstorm. A hunger, or a lack, which might be the same thing. The bed started moving. The fresh air of the corridor. I opened my eyes again. Fluorescent lights blinking in my eyes like a POV music video from the nineties, the ones that played all day long on my mother's television, when she couldn't get out of bed for days. A red door opened and I was deposited in another room. Cool and crowded. Still the blue and the white. Still the fleurs-de-lis patterns. Someone in the bed next to mine was coughing. They coughed and coughed and I felt sorry I wasn't coughing.

You are awake, I thought, as I sheepishly ate the yogurt and bread they handed me on a tray. You are awake. I chewed the bread five times with my teeth on the left side and five times with those on the right. You are awake. But time was still an ambiguous thing, and my pain was still there with me, in a half-hearted, melancholy way, as if what I was experiencing was not pain but the memory of pain. You are awake.

I couldn't feel the numbness now. A more general and more generous lack of sensation had taken its place. The world was blurry and I was out of focus. I thought of a film where a character is literally out of focus and the filming crew is trying to tell him I don't know how to put this but man you are soft. Oh is it my acting, should I try to do it in a different way the actor asked. No man you don't understand you are all blurry. You better sleep it off man. The actor returns home to try to sleep it off and his wife is saying hey, you look different you look a bit unsure of yourself, and his son is chanting, daddy's out of focus daddy's out of focus. That's what it felt like. I was all soft and fuzzy and unnecessarily sweet like smashed pudding. After another while, after my coughing neighbor had been wheeled out in their bed, and I had cleaned my plates, I did some simple math in my head. Then I recited a few poems. Then I vaguely remembered that someone was supposed to be waiting for me. He was waiting for me. So I sat up straight and began to dress, in a half-hearted, melancholy way.

This time I had no trouble getting out because they finally told me how. I pushed open an orange door after a red door. When the orange door opened he was suddenly there, sitting in the lobby with a miraculously hopeful face that I always wanted for myself. Would he ever get lost in a hospital I wondered. Probably not. He was not the type. He began to stand up when he saw me. Have you been waiting long I asked. No he said, not at all, it's okay. We stood face to face and I tried to smile with my numb face. I could tell he was considering whether he should do something for me, carry something for me, make certain things easier for me. I'm okay I said, let's get out of here. Where are we going he asked. I told him where I lived, one of the twin buildings connected by a long bridge. I know where that is he said, that's a nice dorm, new, right? I was happy to let him lead the way and while we walked, I looked at his ankles. Once out of the hospital compound he slowed down to allow me to catch up. I couldn't help looking at him. I asked him questions about himself. He answered with short phrases. Hometown. Major. Dorm. He was born in a small town and that explained his manner of speech, soft and measured. That explained his generosity. The confluence of influences that produced him.

We were at the bus stop at that point and would soon be crossing the quad leading to my room. Is he aware of his beauty? He must be. At a certain phase in our talks Frankie and I were obsessed with people who had that effortless beauty and what we really wanted to know was what a normal day would be like for them. What would it be like to be spared the doubts that imprisoned our thoughts and marked the limits of our experience. To them, everything must feel within reach. All they need to do is to show up. They wouldn't see any *no trespassing* signs anywhere. They probably don't even know signs like that exist. Being white is probably like that, Frankie said, and being beautiful too, maybe. We first had this discussion when we were watching the sorority hopefuls lining up in front of the bus stop to be transported to some distant venue where they would have heart-to-hearts with kindred souls. We had this discussion again when one of our mutual friends, a gorgeous person in my opinion, cried their heart out during a party saying that their biggest regret in college was that they were not beautiful enough. Beauty is a shortcut, Frankie said. Or perhaps it's a license, I said. And let's not forget it's also a social construct she said. No no of course not. We laughed. We lit our cigarettes, another shortcut to pleasure. When I thought about this I really, really wanted to smoke, but I wasn't sure what he would feel about it. You see, I picked up smoking during an era when it was no longer a sign of deep self-examination but a sign of dark self-destruction. For a moment I imagined violently pushing smoke rings into his face and how he might blink slowly in response. He intrigued me. I wanted to do things to alarm him, to distort his nice features. But I didn't feel too keen to offend him just yet. During the entire walk I was conscious that while I was observing him he was also looking at me, and somehow that look was stripped off of him and attached itself to me in order to become a part of me.

We entered the room. My roommate was out, as usual. I sat down on the small futon. He walked past my desk which held the books I was half-reading and the notes I was half-taking and the sentences I was half-writing. He was entirely uninterested in any of that and headed straight to where I was. His lack of interest in the building blocks of my internal world was almost touching. He sat down next to me. He didn't ask me whether I was feeling okay. He didn't say hey, you should probably rest. Like a normal person would. Instead he was patiently exuding his charms in a soft and silent way—what was he thinking? I saw how young he was. The way he would place his one hand upon another and rest his chin on it—what was he thinking? He turned to me and finally asked if I was feeling okay. Yes, I said, I feel wonderful. His eyes lingered on my hair—what was he thinking? After a few minutes he said he liked my hair color. Blue is his favorite color. Really I said, you are not just saying that to make me happy. No I mean it he said. He smiled, in a sweet and conciliatory way—what was he thinking? I asked him if he would like some water, or wine, and then it occurred to me he might be underage. Oh god, I thought. He was still smiling and he shook his head. No I'm good he said. I thought about the first time I heard this phrase. At the time I couldn't understand how you can refuse something by saying I'm good. I refuse, therefore I'm good, or, I'm good, so I must refuse? He looked at me inquiringly. I laughed at myself again.Everything was slightly out of focus. The afternoon sun had slipped through the window and the room was golden. It would remain so for another half an hour this time of the year. My guitar was golden. The mirror was a glistening lake. The poster on the wall turned green.

Children of Paradise. The heroine in that film had said, *love is so simple.*

But sex is simpler. We wrap a tie around the doorknob. Sometimes we use a sock. We wake up and our roommate is cuddling with a guy we've never seen in that single bed of hers and we get dressed in the dark. Before we know anything about sex we already know too much about it. The first day of school when we were progressing towards the stadium for a congregation, someone walking next to me began to tell me how she'd like to take her RA home. I remember how she said it. I'd like to take him home and... and she giggled. She had a quiet voice and she never walked in a straight line. But somehow that made her movements more cat-like. When we walked her shoulder brushed against mine from time to time but that was all. For a few weeks after that she would walk into our room unannounced to talk about the sex she would like to have. The sex that was promised to her. Like the rest of us she believed that on this campus there is a predetermined amount of sex allocated to each one of us according to some algorithm, though we can never be sure what goes into that algorithm. Hence all the gym going, party going, drinking and forgetting and proclaiming to forget. We can't possibly miss any opportunity, however small, to better our chances. She wore make-up every day and could be seen in all the right places. But in the end she had to cry on my roommate's bed for not getting into her preferred sorority. When it was just the two of us in the room, she stopped crying and asked me, hey you are good at math, right? Could you help me with my multivariable calculus? Something was brewing outside our window, a rainstorm or a prelude to a rock concert, which usually produce the same aura or temperature in the air. With our windows wide open I told her that unlike other people who look like me, I'm not good at math. Ah okay she said. The smell of greasy food permeating in the room. Her eyelashes sticking together. Sweat glistening on her arms. We regarded one another. Me in my colorful dress and she in her black tank top. It was already nine in the evening and chances of either of us getting laid this night were negligible, and that's why she was still talking to me. It didn't work the other way around though. We could not just walk into her room unannounced. The door to her room was perpetually closed, with her name written in a cursive hand on a board pinned to the door. Clouds and rivers. I liked her name. She had another name and I wasn't sure if I liked that one as much. A few months later we all found that out. People started playing videos of her on their screens, in their rooms. Soon the entire school knew. Another few months later during my intro-level public policy class the professor was talking about rational ignorance. So, sometimes the cost of acquiring certain knowledge exceeds the benefit that knowledge produces, and in that case it is rational to be ignorant about those things. For example, how many rays does the sun on Uruguay's flag have? Nobody knew. What about the capital of Tajikstan? A few people knew. What is the stage name of our porn star? We all laughed. Another few months later we read an article in our school newspaper where she said she was a feminist. She stated, quote, *rape culture is prevalent. I feel empowered doing this.* People talked about this article with malicious interest for weeks and they read it out loud in various common rooms and coffee shops. A few years later I tried to find that article to see what kind of connection she gave those two statements of hers but the article was 404 not found. As usual my memory outlived that of the Internet. Another few years have gone by and when I finally think about her again people have already stopped talking about her, including herself. It would now be entirely rational to know nothing about her.

The first kiss was with teeth. We kissed until we bled, in a golden moment when my head was still in the clouds and he was the only object I could identify. And I thought: *after this day we would still see each other, by chance or by design.* Somehow it was very erotic, the prospect of seeing him again. We moved towards the bed. I almost laughed because we had to climb onto the bunk bed one after another, imitating each other. I thought: What are we but a mirror invested by the (masculine) subject to reflect himself, to copy himself. I probably thought that just because I felt the need to think of something. What does this remind you of? Then there were more kisses. Kisses fell on skin. The false promise. Remember, the center of a bagel is always fat free. He was closing his eyes. I said things. I told him things, uninvited, in an attempt to lighten things up I guess. I told him about stars and songs. Mountains deep in snow. Meandering country roads leading towards windowless kitchens. Women gathering in one of those windowless kitchens, their fingers full of dried flour. Dried flowers. We put them in liquor bottles on a windowsill. Through the broken window we saw the men in the family, men who each put a cigarette on top of their pouted lips and asked the new bride to fetch it with her teeth. They were saying ridiculously childish things to her. What you would say to a little bird, I imagine.

Oh but you eat like a bird. She was alone in that room in her red qipao with her red lips and red flowers in her hair and we, children, screamed outside the broken window because we thought she was being tortured. We didn't know what was happening but we witnessed on her painted face signs of torture. But the grown-ups assured us, it's all fine; don't you worry. Grown-ups' faces hidden in shadows as children continued to scream. My mother stood in a corner and looked at me, beseechingly. What does she want from me I thought. She wants me to have that life that she could never get. She managed to escape that mountain but stopped at that. I was entrusted to escape the country. Alright. I wanted him to say something. I asked him questions. I wanted to know more about him about how he came to be him. And what this reminded him of. He whispered in my ear that well he didn't have anything interesting to say, but does it feel good. It does I said, and it's fine. Then I thought, the loves I will have and am having. Generations of people who gave their lives to me, quite literally, so that I could have these terrible loves I have. Then I was hungry again, a hunger so unprecedented a hunger even greater than the hunger I felt those days when I didn't eat at all. What's wrong, he seemed to be asking with his eyes. I shook my head.

When I woke up alone in the dark I thought of this sentence, *it eats; I do not*. What is *it*? I turned slightly to the right. There was an imprint of where his body was. Like the erasure of an island from a map that no longer existed. Wet memories. But what is it? The bed smelt of sea salt. *His* smell. The smell of my father after he shaved in the morning. I would re-discover this smell again and again in the wake of my lovers. It eats; I do not. One eats all sorts of things, objects, people, situations, family dramas, political crises, personal rifts, literature, pages and pages. One eats too much that cannot be articulated. But this ambiguous *it*. It might be that which cannot be said. It cannot be said. It, then, is eating; this, then, is a case study. I chuckled in the dark, turning my face to the other side. The meal is not over when I'm full. The meal is over when I hate myself. Who said that? My mother was sitting quietly at the table of men. She was the only one not smoking and the only one not eating. Huge chunks of mutton on bone. Thin-sliced pig ears. Meatballs swimming in oil. My mother watched them with amusement, or bemusement, surrounded by second-hand smoke and second-rate calligraphy. The only college graduate in the family, she had earned her right of not preparing food and still sitting at the table, unlike the other women. I'm not hungry, she said. A plump child not yet introduced to the arts of restraint, I ate. I devoured. Flesh and bones and grease. I caught sparkles of appreciation in their eyes. Years of hunger had taught them to enjoy the spectacle of a child's primordial instincts, which are genuine and unproblematic. They wanted to promise me everything. They promised more than they could ever give, even. They hid those little coins in dumplings and nudged me to pick the one with a coin inside. They were simple, good-hearted people with healthy appetites. I never wanted to go back to that table again.

I was meeting Frankie at a different table. She texted me to say she was too hungover and wouldn't be able to pick me up and she apologized, which caused me to interrogate myself a bit whether I gave off the impression that I took everything for granted. On the way there, the pain woke up. It had some nice rest and was ready to do tricks again, all buoyant and triumphant, like a happy little elf. I tangoed with it with my eyes closed, feeling how it jumped up and down my veins like Pop Rocks. When I got off the Uber at the German pastry shop whose name we could never pronounce, I found Frankie sitting at a table in a white shirt that had a political statement and her blue ripped jeans. We discussed the political statement and I concluded the discussion by saying how sad it was that we were now nostalgic about a time only one year ago. Frankie said yeah, well. Then she flipped the menu over and scrutinized her choices. She carefully considered what kind of things each of them would do to her body. While she did that, I thought about you briefly, the first time in the past twenty-four hours. I was making progress. But when I thought about you I thought about that island where you exiled yourself. What exactly did you say? Oh yes, you were trapped on an island and you were sorry you couldn't share life with others. Finally I knew what I could say in response. I knew I could tell you but you see, we could be an archipelago. But saying that wouldn't really solve the problem would it. I wanted to flip the table over, make some noise, be a nuisance, but it was way too early. Instead I asked for pancakes and a black coffee.

While we waited for food, Frankie said she finally understood where I came from. Where's that I asked. She began to describe to me a party where there was mud and other things on everyone's face. People were naked and behaving badly. She literally got tripped by sweating writhing bodies and fell straight into the mud. It really felt like shit. She showed me videos of her surrounded by beautiful muddy people so beautiful they were like demi-gods that I didn't even know existed on this campus and so muddy it took me a while to confirm that none of them were Asian. Frankie was looking not quite herself in those videos, bewildered, helpless. But that's the thing she said.

I was at this party that everyone wanted to get into but when I was there I felt ridiculous. Yeah I said, that's basically how I feel about everything. Hmm but you handle it with a certain levity Frankie said, like you've seen through it all and you are just playing along. I wanted to point out that she also thought I was intense, but I didn't. The pancakes arrived at our table drenched in syrup. With all that syrup the pancakes were still dry, remarkably dry that they got stuck in my throat like fishbones. I pushed them down with more coffee. The pain got worse with each bite but still I ate with a sense of ceremony, like a person who was smoking and coughing at the same time. I whole-heartedly believed in the death instinct and its small manifestations in everyday life, such as how I'd drink lots and lots of water when I desperately need to pee. For a moment I wasn't sure if it was me or the pain that was eating this pancake. In any event the pain seemed very happy to be nourished.

What is it Frankie said, you're a bit distracted today. I poked at my pancake and said, oh just, I fucked someone. It was a bit random. There, she said, levity. Perhaps, I thought, but then realized I might be saying this, using this precise phrasing, the active voice, to seek her approval. How it even felt like a small victory, me doing things. That I was a doer. That I proved that I, too, could objectify men if I wanted to. What I didn't know was that doing things and letting things happen to you may very well be the same thing. Frankie was cutting her omelet into tiny, manageable chunks. The sound of her knife scratching the plate gave me goosebumps.

Nobody really likes raisins, but somehow they still exist. When I began to write again, my words were looking like raisins, dry, insincere, ashamed. The second they came into being they had to start apologizing for their existence, for taking the space. I felt inadequate for using the portentous we, so I added qualification upon qualification. For instance, *we should be cautious to never let abstraction kill singularity*, I wrote, *or to let a grand narrative suffocate breathing individuals*. When your entire foundation is suspect, you carve your suspicion onto its columns. You remind people who are passing by and marveling at the beautiful beams and windows that this house you see is built on a false premise so don't lean on it. I'm telling you this because I'm honest. And also because to build a house you'll always need some kind of foundation and it's impossible to stand a house upon too many self-contradictions. So I wrote:

> The collectivity we dream does not prevent us from desiring by ourselves, and, from time to time, casting a cold eye on fellow dreamers whose desiring removes or revokes something crucial to our identity. We have to always see each comment, each post, as a single moment for a unique individual with no precedent and parallel, who has their own history and idiosyncrasies, and who is never to be obscured by the amount of data or by the intricacy of theorization. Through all this contention for power in #foodporn, our utmost freedom

as a desiring human is safeguarded, for we should allow ourselves to desire, but at the same time, we should always be ready to be subject to the questioning of our desire by an equally visible and vindicated voice.

I rested my chin in my palm and looked at the sky outside. These were glorious spring days and I hated glorious spring days. Moisture in the air gathered on my lips. Gray vapors, mirrors that are never clean, wounds from random sharp objects. I had my eyes closed for a long time, as if I were sleeping. My memory was getting blunt. I was losing track. I focused on the sound of the graduate student sitting next to me flipping through a journal, one page after another. I counted. One minute a page. As if they were a human clock. I changed my posture a bit, just a bit. My legs were getting numb from sitting cross-legged for too long on this chair. Then I was reminded again by my mysterious ailments to take my pills. This time it was like someone was pulling on my heart strings to ring a bunch of bells. They messed up in the middle of whatever song they were doing and had to start from the beginning, over and over again. I chewed the pills like they were candy. Soon the pain got worse, as if the little person ringing the bells were throwing a tantrum, protesting, frantically pulling all the strings all at once as soon as the medicine began to fall on their head. I had to place a hand where my first few ribs were and rub the area in circles. I closed my eyes, and comforted the little person there, sh-sh-sh-, it's alright. It's just candy. Because nobody else could see this little person jumping up and down inside of me I must have looked ridiculous from the outside, like your typical woeful Victorian woman placinga hand on her chest before she fainted with a sigh. Or perhaps I just looked like a weird person massaging her own breasts in the library.

I thought about him. I realized it was beginning to become a habit, perhaps a bad habit, of thinking about him whenever I was in pain. In a way I was training myself to think about him constantly. I began to draw an imaginary map in my mind. In my imaginary map he was a cartoon version of himself moving slowly. He always walked slowly, which always made me laugh. This afternoon he had a rehearsal, and right then he would be crawling from the little theater back to his room. If I stood up this second and start to walk towards that path I would catch him just in time. If I timed it well I would bump into him quite accidentally on the diagonal path that connects one Gothic building to another. I would hasten my steps. I would be stepping on stone, grass, stone again. When I was finally on that little path I would slow down again, thinking about whether I have, perhaps, miscalculated. But soon I would see him emerge from the arch right opposite. And it would all be good. He would recognize me by the tiniest of nods and I'd be able to forget about everything else for a second, this pain, my heartbreaking thesis. We would walk side by side, with some distance in between, and still we wouldn't say anything to each other. Soon he would swipe me into his dorm building, where upper-class people are usually not allowed. The fact that I had to be invited in would also make me very happy. He would let me walk into his room first, to gain some ground in it first, and he would wait at the door frame, watching me. I would turn and face him, with some distance in between. He would close the door behind him.I would sit on the desk and tell him please help me and of course he would take that as something naughty and walk towards me. My head would be against his window. One second longer, then the second after that. Each second would be accounted for by my acute awareness of the absence of something. All I needed to do then was to stand up from here and begin to do all of those things I had been thinking about. I just had to set one thing in motion and the rest would fall into place, but somehow I wasn't able to stand up.

I checked my phone again. On my screen were all those messages to be opened, considered, taken care of. A few hours ago I told you that my words were beginning to look like dried raisins. You didn't reply the way I thought you would. You said, something like, yes you have put something in the void haven't you. Your reactions were increasingly surprising, alien, inadequate. I was still wearing your jacket everywhere but I no longer understood why I continued to do that. I couldn't remember for what strange reason I had at one time betted my entire existence on your perspective of things. Unaware of it all, or, uninterested in it all, you kept sending me more words. Five days ago

> you said you were stuck in the vortex of truth
> or the cave of truth. Four days ago
> you were knocking on heaven's door
> but realized you still had some distance to go
> which was also fine. Three days ago
> you asked if we were not closer to truth
> what were we close to? Two days ago
> you told me about the spring rains
> that were like flower needles
> and that you began to understand what it means
> to give out everything. Today
> you said the whiskey glass I sent you had already seen
> an entire bottle. I liked how you used the word *see*

but still I didn't feel like replying.

I put my phone face down on the desk and looked away. I would not look at it again this afternoon. I would look at something else. I was sitting next to a wall of photographs with a title in pink: *Our college is for lovers*. Black-and-white photographs of people long dead who were once holding hands and holding each other's gaze in various corners of this campus. The women in those photos had a hazier presence than the men, as if they just happened to be there and weren't sure how long they would need to stay. Ghostly women who would be mainly remembered for being the lovers of famous men, with their eyes eternally fixed on things that did not exist. I looked up the first women graduates from this college, Mary, Persis, and Teresa. Three sisters. They were said to have joined their brother at this institution to better prepare for their careers as teachers. But they didn't really join. What they did was take classes with tutors after the sun had already set, after all the men had already gone who knows where. What would it feel like, going about your life in this Gothic maze knowing that you were never really part of it, knowing that all you were allowed to have were the afterhours. Mary, Persis, and Teresa. Life was much simpler then—there was less hypocrisy. Today all the doors appear to be opening up to us, but even if we do manage to succeed, even if we do squeeze our bodies through one of these doors, it is always with a sense of sacrifice or guilt. We mold our bodies into the shape of the doors until we no longer recognize ourselves and we become doors to be entered. I am a door to be entered. When he touched me I always winced first. I learned to open up only later on, only gradually. We mistook good training for instincts. We mistook torments for possibilities. We mistook pain for pleasure.

Mary, Persis, and Teresa, I sing for you. If I ever finish this thesis I will dedicate it to you, to our fantasies and failures to the mythical promise of wholeness to the long history of desire to all expressive efforts to all those who have been writing and speaking and creating art and striving to fill the emptiness with something, anything, and to each and every burningly experienced little pain cast aside because it refuses to be bound by that container called language.

His other lovers—or admirers—were rarely talked about, only alluded to. I picked up circumstantial evidence. A slight delay in his response. A trace of indifference in his eyes. The word I would use in Chinese would be that word combining the character of idle and the character of slow. Idle, slow, but unmistakable. From time to time the shape of their bodies would emerge in the form of a text message, or several, urgent, text messages. Sometimes during a long afternoon we'd eat chocolate, chocolate they sent him, and he'd show me the little notes that came with the box. I remember feeling nauseated, when I read those words that were not meant for me. My hands began to tremble but then I remembered chocolate was one of the foods that I shouldn't be eating, no wonder. He raised his chin to look at me, trying to see how I was handling all this, perhaps. I gave him a smile. Pretty nice I said, I mean the chocolate. I felt amused, then tired, then disgusted. He held my hand for a long while. Why me, I said. His answer hinged upon some perceived difference. We were discovering each other, according to him. Then we did other things.He practiced his lines and I corrected the mistakes in his essay. I wore one of his shirts and nothing else, then I walked to his closet and looked at his other shirts. I extended my arms to wrap around the best one, that blue shirt. It had the smell of seawater, like all others, and it smelled like him. It smelled more like him than himself. I smelled the shirt as if he were not there.

He leaned against his bed and his arm was dangling from the edge. I had one of his pencils in my hair, which was fading from blue into a grayish blonde. I bit on the end of another pencil.

We made love again. It was very good and I told him repeatedly how good it was. He was doing everything very slowly, meticulously. He did all the right things. The way he did it was so perfect that it almost made me cry. Afterwards, his breaths were smooth and he was on the border of sleep. The light in the room was fading, receding from his profile. My left ear was very close to where his heart was. Skin connected by his heartbeats. In a stupor, I began to see images from other afternoons when I was equally torpid, shapeless, images from his too, they must be his because I never owned a pool, never lay down next to the very edge of my pool, reading, one leg dangling in the water, I never owned a pink floral sofa facing a garden in an inebriated spring, never sank deep in my sofa facing the garden with my eyes fixed on the ceiling fan going its rounds, while unfamiliar curtains slowly swept the floor, all those afternoons when we had no plans to get out of our horizontal positions, him or me, where our consciousness flickered in an approximation of that oceanic feeling, because you see, to get out of that limitless indissoluble thing, to get out of ourselves, is a feat more heroic than all the great epics combined. But we do have to get out of it, eventually, out of that absorbing immensity. We have to get out of it and emerge from ourselves and be independent and social again. I closed my eyes. I tried to dissect time, break time down into tiny morsels, one second, then the next, until I was again fully conscious of its passing, of my passing, until the concreteness of things was salient to me once again, until I finally moved a bit to glance at my phone. God how late it was. In an instant everything, every little particularized sensation rushed back into my body. My chest was numb. My arm too. I realized he was using my arm as a pillow. His fluffy head. I looked at him and thought about the old story where an emperor was so infatuated with his lover he wouldn't want to disturb his sleep, so the emperor cut off the sleeve of his beautiful robe under his lover's beautiful head. I could do that too. I could chop off my arm. I would chop it off and plant it in soil so when the next spring comes my arm would become a tree, turning new leaves. He would be walking by and seeing that young tree he would finally be reminded of the many sacrifices I made for his soundless little sleep. I removed my arm from below his neck, as quietly as I could. I got out of bed, got dressed, stopped at the door. I turned to look at him again. Half turned, in fact. My body and my eyes were facing different directions. In his sleep he looked even younger and paler. So pale, you, I thought. So pale. Like you were bleached by the sun. I heard something drop, with a colorless sound as colorless as my desire for you, the laughable, stubborn desire I had for you, a desire I never knew. All these colorless little desires that were belatedly taking on their hues. I would still do many things to please you, I thought, it is inevitable.

I closed the door behind me and walked down your hallway trying not to catch anyone's eyes. I felt something soft and fluffy (like your head) under my feet and I looked down to find, to my surprise, that I was stepping on wood, not cotton balls. I quickened my steps.

I made an effort to reorient myself. To readjust my breaths. I had to get my things from the library first and then take the bus to my advisor's office, yes, yes. I was irrevocably late. On my way to the bus stop I could still feel the traces you had left on me and thought about whether they were obvious. One of the tragedies in life is that we could never really smell ourselves. At the bus stop I decided to light a cigarette. After all it would be more decent to smell of tobacco than to smell of sex. As I lit that utilitarian cigarette I felt very bad for allowing myself to succumb to a tiny betrayal, but a betrayal to what, I had no idea.

On the bus I sat down at one of the seats in the front, facing the window. The surest sign of spring was that of a tiny green worm who was hanging on to a piece of what seemed to be spider silk, connected to the window frame. The little worm was curled up and was swaying back and forth quite dramatically in the wind. He was resilient, this little worm. He wouldn't let go. I looked away because I couldn't bear seeing him fall, because he would, eventually. I looked away and started checking my emails. I opened up a document on my phone before I was fully prepared. What popped up on my screen was something bloody, a whole lot of redness being sucked into what looked like a hole, with different angles of a passage. What I saw were images of my interior, damaged, shattered, fragmented. I read the accompanying texts that were supposed to offer some explanation. Run-on sentences. In a measured tone. The issue was not evident, the solution non-existent. I closed that file.

Damaged, shattered, fragmented, I was only able to put all my pieces together when I stepped into his office, my sanctuary. My advisor lifted his eyes from the pages, as he began to say, so, between last night and this a.m. I read over the latest files you sent. Excellent. This is terrific work. I pretended I didn't hear that. Instead I asked him what he thought about my bold engagement with Luce Irigaray's work, of how the imagery of the *two lips* could displace the phallus and how the other two lips could, perhaps, also do that.

Then I digressed. I was saying how the One is so overrated and should be discarded because you see, in a model where the One is indispensable, a woman has to be a lack, an atrophy, a hole. She has to be. But perhaps the insistence on this Oneness is misplaced, perhaps our desire could be *plural*, in a sense that we are irreducible to numbers, neither one nor two, perhaps we don't have to be one or the other at all. I gathered from his expression that he thought it all very cute. He smiled, he smiled while staring at that one image I had carefully chosen for the chapter, the image of an egg and cheese sandwich in an obscene outburst, with the caption *this sandwich was the only thing that kept me wanting more while at an all-girls high school*, and taking all that in he nodded, he nodded and he said, well, it feels like you're still a bit unsure about the shape of this. I don't mean it critically, only that, I'm hoping, perhaps selfishly, to see more of *you* in this. More of me, I thought. Isn't that too much to ask? But if it's him asking then it couldn't be too much to ask. Yes, sure, there are many things I could talk about, many things I could add. For instance, the burden as well as the freedom of constructing identities, linking our self-image to our consumptive behavior, equating ourselves with the food we like. For instance, the loosely-organized taste community in which taste is socially recognized and validated through tagging and sharing and commenting. For instance, those undercurrents of resistance,the valorization of street food, home-made cuisines, and other items not conventionally associated with prestige, in an effort to counterbalance the elite food producers occupying all those Michelin restaurants. Wait, I could even talk about how, in fact, seeking pleasure in consuming the virtuality of food while so many others are suffering from true hunger is in itself a display of privilege, one that involves political exploitation common to traditional sex porn. It was there he had to stop me. He said, that's all very good, but what I meant was, why, why were *you* interested in this project in the first place? I never asked. Of course you don't have to answer if it's too personal. Because, I said, because I know it's true. It's all true. I know it's true because I also starve myself. Then say it, he said.

I opened my mouth. I put in a cigarette. From the outside the gallery at dusk looked like floating clouds, floating clouds with humans inside, moving and reshaping all very quickly. People in twos and threes who dressed so differently from all the other people in this town but so similarly to each other, like they were photoshopped. Tote bags and big earrings and very red lipsticks, red like wine, red like fresh blood and their colorful bandanas and their long socks, their straight jeans and their platform oxford shoes. I walked by the gallery once, twice, carrying my matches, glancing through the window. Nobody seemed to notice. They were holding beers and brochures and holding each other's gaze. I walked to the other side of the street and stood next to the cane chairs of a permanently closed bistro, watching the people in that glass cage who could not hear me even if I screamed, I was sure. There really wasn't a room in this town that was meant for me. I was about to call an Uber to flee the scene, but then I saw that the twos and threes in the gallery were splitting up and forming some semicircle facing a wall. I put my phone back into my pocket and began to cross the street.

Many people were dancing around when I pushed the door open. I made sure that the wall I was about to lean on did not have any artwork on it and at the same time put more pills into my mouth. The dancing people started to chant. It was supposed to be poetry I believe. I heard: something something clouds, somebody somebody screams. Bridges, horses, villages, knuckles, mothers, a death, a chill, the usual. Then I ate. At these events you could always count on the presence of food to prevent us from talking to one another. Finger food. Medicine-sized food. As long as I timed it well I could manage to keep this food down for several hours, but I knew only too well how unstable the whole system was and how chewing without concern was, really, a luxury, so I allowed myself to get carried away a little before anything that would happen happened, enabling other things that could happen. I chewed. Mini crab cakes and potato chips and sausage rolls. By this point my palate was hyper-sensitive to sugar and oil, burdened, defeated, embarrassed by their lingering gravity. I put half-bitten pieces onto a black napkin and carefully folded the napkin several times and crushed it in my fist.

The artists continued to dance. They seemed happy, functional. I was drawing in huge amounts of air and, conscious that I was taking air away from others, feeling guilty about my needs. While I was still measuring my breaths the dancing people vanished into shadows, and someone else stepped into the spotlight to introduce the films. A young woman with side bangs, a round face, and a soft voice. Seeing her I thought about what Frankie once told me. She said she knew she would never be American because she could never get a quick read of a person she just met here. With people from China she could. Before the person even opened their mouth she would understand, from the way they dressed, the way they moved their bodies, among other more invisible traits, their socioeconomic standing. After they spoke just one sentence she knew where their hometown was, approximately, when they left China, and what they were doing with their lives. After five minutes she would know everything she needed to know about them, their likes and dislikes and insomnias and idiosyncrasies. But she could never have that tacit understanding of an American, not even her close friends. She never knew what they were thinking. It was like they were birds she said. Frankie was terrified of birds because she never knew what birds were thinking. She would look at them—her American friends I mean, not birds—and get confused for a moment because she felt she couldn't even identify their species. Americans are a total mystery to her and would remain that way. Good thing is, I thought, that they love to flap their beautiful wings to distract you from thinking about what they actually are. And right then, when this young woman began to speak, I knew what Frankie meant. I understood this woman immediately. I didn't know her at all but I understood her. Within seconds I understood she was from a northern town in China and only moved here one or two years ago, that her middle-class family was studious and wordless, that they would be wordlessly taking a family photo or making dumplings. Bamboo mats, mosquito nets, fans shaking their heads. That people in her town gossiped a lot and they would say to each other that she had the kind of face that would eventually kill her husband. But she never wanted a husband. What she wanted was to get out of there. Now, with a familiar and almost endearing accent she was saying things like blurred boundaries, the history of deterioration, and how the world is being worlded. She was hanging onto those words with all her mightto get as far as she could from her wordless family and her wordless small-town life. I understood that. Like her, I was hanging onto the brochure made of recyclable brown paper to get away from these thoughts. Among the abstract shapes on that brown paper was his name, the name I had tried to write onto a wine glass some weeks ago.

A few minutes later I took a picture of the brochure in my hand though I wasn't planning on sending it to anyone or looking at it ever again.

The lights were off. After a few freeze-frames of a smoky northern town in China credits began to roll. And I had a sudden impulse to cry, to bawl, to scream, to pull off my hair, to become your stereotypical hysterical woman and to do it with my entire soul. I didn't. Instead I rolled the brochure into a phallic shape. Hey, relax, I thought. I have to see the film. That's why I'm here. I have to see it so as to convince myself that his creation is as worthless as my love for him. But as usual I didn't really see the film. The film rolled on and my eyes were elsewhere. What I kept seeing was him holding the camera, walking past some exposed pipes and fallen billboard, him in a traveling black beanie. What I kept seeing was the childhood he never talked about, with death sitting in the corner of the room, watching him. What I kept seeing was a particular turn of phrase he liked, translated into images. It's never a good idea to know the creator before seeing a piece of art because their face and their handprints would be all over the art, defacing their art, handcuffing their art. For a moment I thought I was with him in that room, watching the doorknob, because he once told me doorknobs were important to him in an inexplicable way, and he would stare at one for an entire afternoon. I do that too, I said. Of course you do, he said. Our fixations were nameless and strange, and nobody else would know this. Nobody in this small projection room at least. So we stood side by side and watched together. During that brief moment when there was only him and me and the doorknob in the room, the sense of safety I felt was boundless. But as soon as the lights were on and other people began to try to explain him to me,

I just wanted to get out of there as soon as possible.

At times it seems impossible to understand what is really happening. Things slip through my fingers like sand. Now that's a lazy metaphor and not entirely accurate. It's more like I'm a hollow portal that people and events pass through absent-mindedly. That's somewhat more accurate, but just as lazy. Around the time I saw his film I decided to make an effort to re-connect to experience. To start small, I would listen to a song carefully, from start to finish. Yes, I would immerse myself in each second of it. Because a song, or music in general, is an artform entirely in time, about time, of time, unlike any other. I did that with songs I was already familiar with, even though I knew how it would go, how it would get there from here. But let's try to truly experience it shall we? Let's try to be in it. Let's try to be it, I thought to myself whenever I started from the beginning. But soon, in the middle of it all, I would lose track. I got distracted by a sight or a thought and the song receded to the background. When the attention, or the determination to attend, returned, the song had already progressed to another verse without me noticing. And I'd come to a stop, extremely annoyed with myself, and re-start from the beginning. With a song I could do that. But with a person I could not. I could not say to them, hey I lost a beat, can we rewind a bit, or even better, can we start from the beginning. What had happened to me when I was not paying attention was lost forever. I lost half of my life like that already. And as I was thinking about all this you already moved on. What I had done in between I had no idea. By then we were already familiar with each other, so familiar that we had a kind of script, or a recipe, with each little step pre-written, tested. *I'm so obsessed with food that I look up recipes for things I would never make!* Oh the many similarities between manuals on sexual techniques and manuals on the preparation of food—the same untiring emphasis on the ultimate delight. The same artificiality and unattainability. You were oblivious to all of this and you whispered to me. You asked, hey do you want me to give you… No! I screamed before you even finished your sentence, horrified. No no no I said, no! Oh okay you said. I saw the shape of your momentary confusion. You kissed me on my cheek and resumed the script, or recipe. I turned my head to the left and saw something very dirty on the carpet. I tried not to see it. And I thought, in the end there is still unsuspected filth abandoned to life. Your head was on my shoulder and I bit my lips to not make a sound. I could feel your eyes on me. I could feel your attention turning into droplets of rain brushing against each part of my body. Everything about me was miserably seen on this endless floor. I covered my face with my palm.

You were just trying to be nice. I told myself, you were just trying to be nice, then why was I horrified? Was it because by saying that you were reminding me that you, too, have a mouth. The two lips, the unsituated pleasure that I was constantly musing over is not mine alone. You have a penis and you have a mouth too. You would put things into your mouth too. You could tuck into a pizza, shovel into a tub of ice-cream, slurp up pasta, luxuriate in whipped cream, bite off half a bun. I had forgotten about that. I had even forgotten about the time when I told you it was my birthday, and you brought out these ugly red balloons and tried to fill them up one by one with your breaths. Injecting air that traveled through your lungs into those limp balloons as I watched you do that, and I was still watching when you had to let the balloon go, finally, because you decided, much to your chagrin, that you couldn't tie it up, and the balloon was making a desperate farting sound while darting this and that way throughout the room and we were laughing our heads off, even then I had forgotten that you have a mouth.

Before you left, before you finally were about to leave I asked you whether you could stand next to me for a bit while I smoked. You said yes sure. We got out from the back door and stood in the parking lot. You were checking your phone for the time of the next bus that would bring you back to your part of the world. I took out one chocolate-flavored cigarette and lit it. You did not walk away but you did not ask for one either. From time to time a car stopped in front of us and a few girls in high heels and very short skirts packed themselves into it. I smoked with a determination to savor each rush to the head. Then I forgot about this cigarette as I began to notice that you were looking at me with, what is it, compassion? I was still a bit annoyed with you, for whatever reason. Perhaps it was envy. I envied that you didn't have to smoke and you never had to say anything. So I said, perhaps it's best we stop seeing each other. Why you said. I'm graduating I said, and I need to focus on my thesis. That was the first thing that came to mind, but I wasn't sure if it was true. After I said that I realized I smelled of you. I buried my face into my own sleeves and it was you. Several weeks later when I was really graduating and moving out I would light all the candles that Frankie gifted me at one time or another like I was exorcizing something. Then I would resume packing and as the candles continued to burn I would gradually realize that all the candles had your smell. I would think about whether I should tell you, when I looked at the labels of those candles and identified the scent, whether I should tell you hey you know what you smell of sea salt and sage. I didn't. And while you were still standing next to me you looked at me with a certain intensity. But I like you very much you said.

It was only when you were really gone that I began to cry, for whatever reason. I cried soundlessly so that I wouldn't surprise myself. I buried my entire face into the pillow which an hour ago had held your head and cried into your scent. Blood and semen and sweat and tears. Then I sat motionless for a while at my desk. After that I printed out pictures from my endoscopy and placed them side by side with my pictures of food. I was delighted by some facile similarity between the inside of my digestive system and those extreme close-ups of raspberries. Both are smooth and pink and fragile, bathing in a delicious lighting. Both are obscene. The raspberries are truly sexy, though. Some wind got into the room and the pictures swayed and jostled. Like one scene from his film. Some parts of his film reminded me of Chris Marker. Other parts of it reminded me of home-made videos. The rawness he was seeking was too carefully manufactured. Either too good or too bad. He, of course, has long decided to never be mediocre. And one day, looking at those pictures I thought, I would send these pictures of rawness to him in a beautiful envelope with dried cherry blossoms. I would write on the envelope, a piece of me. Then he would be looking at them without knowing what he was looking at, feeling a slight discomfort nonetheless. I had no idea why I would want to do that.

My roommate was back in the room now, pacing around, picking out clothes for her next big thing. She glanced at the pictures. What are these she asked. Are you looking at pictures of a vagina? Nope, I said. She placed her backpack on her chair. Then she sat on her desk with her legs dangling. I was still gazing at the pictures and she had to look at them as well. The scent of blood semen sweat and tears in the room. She cleared her throat and said, so I've been voice messaging this random guy, and he would say the craziest things. Filthy things. Like what I asked. She jumped off her desk and began to play a voice message for me. A deep hoarse voice was saying: *It's raining outside and I will catch you at the staircase, pin you against the wall. I will rip off your clothes and bite into your nipples. How you writhe and beg for me and I will give it to you. I'll drive my dick into your little cunt and smooth out all the folds and cuts in it.* The voice message was cut off at that. Yeah, she said. There were many more and she played them for me one by one. Why did she feel the need to do that? I don't know. Perhaps because the room smelled of sweat blood and semen and she had to reinstate herself. Meanwhile I was fascinated by how the deep hoarse voice had said *folds and cuts*. Folds I understand, but where do these cuts come from? The convenient metaphor of our vagina as a wound, no doubt. Cuts produce a lack, to be filled up by pain. Hairs standing up on a raspberry. My internal writhing. It was raining outside. I closed my eyes and together we listened to his imaginary moans again and again.

After I saw the doctor again about those fresh pink pictures, he gave me some new medicine called proton pump inhibitors, which sounded very inhibitive and pompous. I asked the doctor how this would actually work and he said it would neutralize the acid that was supposedly too much in me. I have too much acidity in me? Yes he said, way too much, and we would try to reduce it, like I said (as he circled out a few of those photos that were supposed to mean something to me). I nodded. I took the new pill once in the morning and once before bed without fail but whenever I was lying down, like now, the excess was still keenly felt, along with my feeble attempt at containing it, flowing in all directions. I asked Frankie whether she ever felt that her body was streams and rivers, and she told me no it felt more like a salt lake. That must be a good feeling I said.

We were lying down on the grass in the garden. Not too far away from us was the red Japanese temple, a distant cousin of those little temples my grandfather spent his whole life building in that village in the mountains. I wondered why I began to think about things in that village a lot more often recently, probably also a way to reinstate myself. Frankie was wearing proper spring attire today. Pastel blue and soft yellow. Rays of sun. I asked her how her thesis was going. Oh thank god it's nearly done she said. That's great I said. I turned to the left and buried my cheeks in blades of grass. No, not blades of grass, silk of grass.

When it was proper spring the grass was so soft that you felt you would melt in it. Your entire body was a huge cotton candy. We watched the ducks in the lake, discussing why they were behaving that way. We had half-eaten bagels and half-drunk black coffee and half-finished drafts on our laptops. We had massive amounts of time on our side. I kept my body on my side to ease the pain because when we are lying on one side we only feel half of our body and very logically, half of the pain. Sauce on the side, please. And then we never touch it. Everything put to the side is already reduced to a nice thought. A moment later Frankie asked what about you, how's your writing going. And I told her that I couldn't go on. Well to be very honest I couldn't write a single word. She seemed surprised and concerned. We watched the ducks some more.

It felt like my heart was burning. Not only that. My entire being was aflame. The little person living inside me was setting fire to everything and while they were at it the little arsonist was probably also standing at the edge of some organ smoking with a straight face observing the end of their world as they knew it. Breathe, I thought. From the corner of my eye I saw that Frankie was sitting up again, chewing on her bagelwhile looking at pictures of food on her phone. I would get up soon as well, I thought. I began to play a little game with myself. If I were still burning in five minutes I would get up and walk towards the lake and drown myself quietly. I would pick up little stones to put in my pocket and then step into the lake. I wondered if the bottom of the lake had a nice slope so that I could let myself gradually disappear into it. It was reassuring that I didn't know how to swim. Frankie was asking me hey why are you touching your stomach like that are you feeling okay?

I told her that I was trying to find some pockets. You don't have pockets on this dress Frankie said. Yeah, right, is that why women's clothes usually have fewer pockets than men's? I don't know what you might be thinking, she said, but don't think that.

I squinted at her in the sun. On this day she was devoid of shadows. The sun had forgotten about us, I thought. Frankie picked up her phone again to look at Snaps. At the same time, she was describing to me in detail what she would like to eat later. Lately she had this thing where she would put the word big before each noun. She would stress the *big*, in Chinese, followed by the name of the food in English, and because *big* in Chinese is *Da* it always sounded extravagant, even a bit deviant. For instance she would tell me she was dying for a Da ice-cream. Da chicken wings. Or a Da soda. Right then she was going on and on about some Da cavatelli pugliese from a new restaurant that was, can you believe this, called Mothers & Sons. Sounds great I said. Then, without looking at me Frankie said, you know, this little lover of yours, I dig not. Hmm I don't think I told you who it is I said. Well, she said, he's been telling everyone. Oh I said. Yeah he was saying many things, Frankie said, unpleasant things too. I stared at the ducks who were putting their heads into the water, looking for food I guess. And I thought how lucky these ducks could just stick their heads into water and hide for a while and it would be perfectly socially acceptable. Then Frankie said, by the way, at one of the parties I saw him, your little lover. I'm not surprised I said, he seems to be everywhere. So yeah, Frankie said, we were playing a game, Truth or Dare or something, and at a certain point he took off his shirt. And? I asked. Well she said, I think you can do much better. Ha ha, I said, of course. I closed my eyes and thought about what that body looked like, your body. No, I won't think about you. I will think about how our bodies have been transformed into an instrument and a product, and see, our competence in terms of cultivating our bodies can be converted into capital, both economic and sexual. What an emotionally demanding process. I knew you were one of those people whose bodies are routinely inspected and inventoried. But still it isn't good enough. It's never good enough. No I will not think about you. I will think about how we are asked to concurrently maximize our consumptive behavior while exhibiting self-control. That's why food porn must first acknowledge this degradation so as to deploy shame in the service of pleasure. A degradation. No I won't think about that. An idealization and a degradation at the same time. No. Meanwhile Frankie was again talking about that restaurant called Mothers & Sons. Yes. So, we would go to this new place. And there we'd order only the antipasti and the primi, never the secondi. We'd skip the dessert, because summer was lurking around the corner, you see. Good plan I said. The pain was blurring my vision. I closed my eyes and thought again about drowning myself. Whenever I close my eyes one of us would get killed, I thought.

I started to work on an ending in my head. various people had warned me that I should never work on the ending prematurely, but at that moment it seemed drastic measures were called for:

> #Foodporn—as object, practice, aesthetics, cultural capital, and community—is sexy because the satisfaction of nutritive needs is the primordial pleasure ever imprinted on us

> much as seeing is, in essence, pornographic.

It is sexy because in its richest and most lustrous form, it is transgressive;

it rebels against the dominant discourses restricting our appetite, even if the very virtuality of this mode of consumption manifests our acquiescence to such discourses—ever intertwined with patriarchy, neo-liberal ideology and capitalism—concerning the self-regulation of health and body image.

It is sexy because it is always there but never present, an empty promise of the retrieval of the lost object, itself restricted by the impotency of symbolization, an inherent limit of jouissance.

It is sexy because it allows us to imagine a pleasure sans human objects, but we are also always part of a diverse community of fellow "addicts" and ensuing power dynamics, where we reassure each other that we are never alone.

It is sexy because it gives us (the women) a new path to subversion, with its pleasurable potential and erotic possibilities.

That was not it at all. All wrong. To make it right again we need to get going. We need to go somewhere. So, we would go to this restaurant. And then we'd order only the antipasti and the primi, never the secondi. Frankie would be frantically tapping her phone and looking at Snaps, with captions starting with "just," "typical," or "your" and ending with "hmu" or "lmk." She would say to me hey let's hit this place. Sure I would say, taking a last bite of my pasta drenched in oily squid ink, knowing that I probably shouldn't. Soon we would arrive at a place where there would be music on speaker phone and a lot of skin. Soon we would be getting ourselves into some ridiculous game. Frankie would be well at ease, as always, at the center of everything, directing our attention towards different corners of the room so that the temperature would always be balanced. Soon I would be kissing someone while standing on a table, someone who just happened to be there. Something in my chest would be pounding with such determination. So loud. Don't be so loud, I would say to it, quiet down don't disturb the others. Then I would be seeking Frankie's eyes while still kissing the random person who just happened to be there. For some reason I need her to see me like that. I need her to see the ugliness in me, the vulgarity. I need her to denounce me, to pardon me, and to still choose to see the good in me. I need all of it. Each step is essential. And when finally I did see her I would begin to feel entirely out of proportion. I would feel that I'm too big for this place. That I am enormous. The tables are barely reaching my ankles or my little toe. That my arms are so long so very long that they could reach through the window and start shuffling the tiny cars on the street and picking up random people so that I could have a good look at them because when you are enormous everything looks really really far away. The world is really far away when you can pick the world up with your thumb and index finger just like that, when your fingerprints are the world, when you are no longer you, when you are the world, when you are usurping the world and the world is devouring you. Then you will completely disappear. You will no longer be. That will be the end of it.

But right then we still had our toes in the grass and our eyes closed, so it was all good. Frankie in her pale blue see-through shirt was still looking as fresh as the first morning on earth. Every few minutes or so she said something in a lazy, sun-drenched voice. I responded intermittently. If it could only be like this, always. Just Frankie and me.

If only neither of us would ever have any intention of moving away from where we were.

I was just walking. I walked past those Gothic buildings and people began to emerge from various big wooden doors at the exact same time in a Kafkaesque sort of way while I continued to repeat to myself *it eats; I do not.* It was three forty-five in the afternoon, a time still too early for everything and already too late for anything. I was walking back to my dorm after my final class of the day, of the semester, and of my college years, in fact, but at the time it didn't feel momentous at all. I was just walking. And when I walked from the parking lot to the little path that would lead me to a group of more Gothic buildings I finally remembered that I first saw this sentence from a food blogger who had an eating disorder. Yes yes, I thought, that's right. Then say it, my advisor had said. I opened my mouth again. There is something vulgar in the act of eating, no? Our jaw moving left and right up and down and even though we have our mouth politely shut, the way civilization has trained us, we all know what's happening, don't we, that the beautiful tuna and beef and salad are turning into a ugly mushy thing in between our teeth to be transported down our throat towards our stomach where an even more disturbing process is going on. By eating we are creating waste. But when we are only looking at food it's all very romantic. When I am watching you from afar, for instance, when you are on stage, or when you are just passing by, unaware, unsuspecting, you are all the wild promises.

I have overused the word *promise* in my writing haven't I? Just like when we look at pictures of food we are eating and not eating at the same time, when I looked at you from afar, I was having you and not having you at the same time. And now, what we have is a disorder of sorts. Food porn gets to be porn because eating has become a dirty word. After all, our passion is the passion for emptiness. We eat the void, a non-edible void, an infinite devouring. The rawness of the real, beyond the pleasure principle. My steps had taken me through the quad where people were feeding, handing each other mini tarts and pizza slices. I imagined you giving out pieces of me in a dingy room to another, likely another girl, of you peddling second-hand vignettes, proof of my malice and my desperation, and of the two of you laughing over it together together and together together and I couldn't even remember when I had given you those things of mine for safekeeping. Crumbs from crusty bread fell all over the grass and blue birds flew down from the branches eager to pick up the little pieces. Indeed, you are what you eat. They say the woman is not a signifier that can be articulated; they say the woman is something that is unsaid, an absence-word, a hole-word. The anorexic subject, who signifies nothing, eats nothing. By consuming food porn visually, she is feeding, and appeasing, the object-cause of desire, whilst her emptiness is intact, because, *I do not.* To her, to us, *nothing*, is the thing, the real thing that is forever inadmissible to simplification, that is outside of language. What I have gladly given you is equally incapable of signifying anything. We are good, I thought, then I considered whether it was another piece of evidence of my desperation. That I was doing this little exercise in my mind simply to not feel betrayed or belittled by you. But even that is totally fine.

We should all learn to be a bit more charitable towards ourselves. Do what you need to do. Do what you have to do. And most importantly, do what you want to do. And what is that? When I reached my dorm and saw you standing at the back door, *again*, with both hands in your pockets, my state of mind had become one where I would literally drive my nails into your skin and never let you get away from me. How are you today I asked. I would rip things apart and swallow them whole. I wanted flesh and bone. Okay, you said. I wanted you to fall into pieces and pierce through my organs like knives. Okay how about you, you said.

You didn't move, though, just as I was opening the door for you. You said, in your usual faint voice, that there was a play you'd like to show me. A rehearsal of a play, in fact. Would I be interested? You want me to go to a play with you, I said. A rehearsal, yes, you said. Oh sure I said, I don't have anything urgent. I said that but in fact I had many many pages waiting to be written. You waited there after I said sure, as if you were giving me a chance to change my mind. I smiled at you. Then you were calling an Uber while I quickly typed my lingering thoughts into a new note. You watched me do that. Or perhaps it didn't happen this way. Perhaps when I opened the door for you you slipped in quietly. Then we did one thing after another in my room, as usual. Then I said your name again and again and that had embarrassed me, as usual. To this day I wasn't sure whether we did it before I lit a cigarette while we waited for the Uber. Perhaps it didn't matter. The day was wet and sultry. Smoke got trapped in my windpipe. I coughed. You looked at me with some concern and I shook my head. Then I said you know for the longest time I thought a windpipe is a musical instrument, like a bagpipe, or a wind chime, or the child of a bagpipe and a wind chime. You laughed almost inaudibly. Once we were in the car there was a brief moment when I didn't feel anything at all, and I was so confused that I turned left and right to see if I had left my feelings behind, somehow. You didn't seem to notice and you asked me what my plans were after graduation. I didn't feel like elaborating on the logistics but then there seemed to be nothing of importance I could say instead. I couldn't tell you it was terrifying me that I was not feeling anything, so I began to tell you all the logistics. And while I mindlessly rambled on I was also trying to summon up all the demons I felt sure were still dormant somewhere inside of me, calling upon them to please please make some noise as this is way too quiet. As long as there was something going on, some movement or revolt down there, I would somehow feel better in believing that interesting things were still happening while we were talking about the most uninteresting details of our trajectories away from each other. I was saying to you, the beginning of May, that's when I'd go back to China. Ah so soon, you said. We were passing by April already. Then we passed by a town that was gray and green at the same time. From the streets nothing could be read. I saw the path I took during my first year when I tried to find the history museum near some abandoned railway tracks, where I would spend an entire afternoon trying to understand what had happened here without my involvement. Then I saw the bar where, a few weeks ago, I sat with my History professor, who over several drinks told me about the things he once did in my hometown. During the eighties he was there to give a speech. During the day he would speak prearranged words to a room of expectant faces and at night he would visit one of the hidden gems in a dingy alley in the French Concession.

Once, he was discussing the Civil Rights Movement with another scholar friend of his. The days were cooling down and they drank Shaoxing wine. Halfway through the night a man from the next table joined them. They ate wontons and talked about poetry, politics, philosophy, until daybreak. I asked him, did this man speak English with you? Well of course, he said. He said everybody spoke English in Shanghai during the eighties. I asked him what that little shop was like. He said it was just around the corner, very ordinary. I didn't believe him. I said no shop would open till daybreak. He said (now he was taking another sip of his whiskey sour), every shop opens until daybreak in Shanghai. Are you really from there? I said, well maybe I'm not. I said it good-humoredly but afterwards I managed to make myself feel quite miserable somehow. It couldn't be that I was not part of this place and I was not part of that place and what was called History was something I couldn't recognize. It doesn't make sense.

You looked at me and asked me what I was looking at. History, I said, history that includes me out. Your eyes twinkled (I really saw it) as you turned and nodded at the same time. I looked out of the window so as not to see that you were not looking at me.

Then you turned back to me and you asked, hey, what's your take on open relationships?

Why, I said (I was in desperate need of a smoke so I might have sounded grumpy).

So a friend of mine is asking if. . . well, but I don't know.

Oh, I said.

The very first time you told me something about your own life and what I said in response was, *but it's none of my business.*

Ha, right, you said.

I might still be holding some unnamed grudge against you,

I wasn't sure. But then I discovered what the problem was, why I was in such a terrible mood. It was only after we got out of the car that I discovered I had been bleeding. I was wearing a white dress that day and blood was dripping down my legs. It wasn't yet the time to bleed. But again when is it a good time to bleed? I entertained the idea of just letting myself go. Let it bleed. I'd sit quietly with you and bleed until I turned white and the theater turned red.

But of course I didn't. I excused myself, as gracefully as I could, and headed towards the restroom. It was not the tame, meager blood you'd see on a first day. No, I was giving out so much blood that I couldn't quite understand it, blood of such a vibrant red and the doctors told me that I was anemic. Or perhaps being anemic doesn't mean your blood is pale. I put a sanitary pad over the red. White on red. I was shaking, or trying to make myself shake a little, to inject some emotion into the situation.

When I walked back into the theater I found you sitting at the very back, even though there were just the two of us. Before the play started we looked around at things without saying anything to each other. During the play I had my arms arched upon my lap and my chin placed upon the back of my hands, leaning forward. I tried to concentrate on the play and pretended that you were not there with me. I tried to let you believe that I was forgetting about you. I was forgetting about you. The actor on stage was enveloped in a massive amount of white gauze. She looked like someone who really believed in herself, as in, she believed in the inevitability of everything, including her dancing around looking like an open wound. A mouth is often described as an open wound. The other two lips, too. I placed a finger on my lips. They were parched.

You put one hand on the back of my neck, putting some slight pressure on that one piece of protruding bone.

The play continued and your fingers wouldn't leave.

My heart was disappearing.

When the play ended you walked towards the actor in white gauze and talked to her. You had your arms folded in front of your chest and you were lowering your head as she whispered into your ear. I walked out of the theater to smoke. I watched the trees and birds for several minutes. Then I realized no smoke was getting into my lungs no matter how hard I sucked on it until I saw that the cigarette was broken in the middle. I lit it again. It was remarkably bright outside and I thought about a poem saying things like children who were born during the day must have done that on purpose and for some reason all I wanted to do at that moment in that immaculate brightness was to talk to him again. Simply talk to him. Him and no one else. Or take a walk with him in the sun. Him and no one else. So I could ask him, do you remember that old poem, the one about how the spring is so very beautiful in Luoyang, but talented youth from Luoyang are still in exile and growing old elsewhere. Yes of course, of course he knew the poem, and he would say something like, history is hurt, and so are we; we hurt each other. I would understand half of it, as usual, but I would understand him, and I would say, yes yes. I would say yes yes yes. My whole being is yes. It would matter little to me that were he to stand by my side at this moment his gaze would fall on me with the same weight as it would fall on the grass and the trees and the birds. It wouldn't matter.

I don't know for how long, but you had been standing next to me. I saw very clearly for the first time you didn't like the fact that I smoked. A little frown, which I had always thought was a facial expression only possible in books. I did catch it there in between your brows. Perhaps it was a literary frown. You looked to the other side.

I killed that cigarette under my feet and threw the butt into a trash can.

You turned around again.

Then you were looking at your feet. You always wore sneakers.

I asked you what you were thinking about.

You said, you scare me a little, do you know that?

Really I said, why is that?

You didn't answer.

Is it because my hair is blue? I thought.

You were looking up at the trees.

I was about to call an Uber. I asked you whether you were hungry. You said not really but you could eat. I picked a restaurant downtown. When we were in the car, the silence seemed to have acquired its own personality so that I felt I should probably give it a name. The car window was slightly open and I was closing my eyes to avoid the dust.

Then I did a thing where I tried to reconstruct your face in my mind with my eyes closed: at first it was pure darkness. Darkness so dark that everything could comfortably melt in it. Not yet. It had to go very slowly. Slow down. I rested my hand on my closed eyelids. And then I began to see you in fragments. Cheekbone. Forehead. Eyebrows. I was avoiding your eyes. I was afraid of what I might find there. Instead my innocuous glances traveled down to your bare arm, pale, ivory. Golden hairs in the sunlight. Pores. I re-opened my eyes and looked at you: it occurred to me that the image I kept in the back of mind didn't match reality.

As soon as we arrived at the restaurant I ordered a cocktail and finished it very quickly. I ordered for you. Oysters as a starter and lobster gnocchi as a main. I had no recollection of what I ordered for myself. It's not important. It was all for you. While we waited for food I ordered another drink and told myself to drink that one fast too. Perhaps I was doing all that to scare you even a bit more. You were not looking at me. Your eyes were on the wooden patterns of the table, then the napkins, then the candlelight. Orange spots were hopping in your eyes like a sacrificial fire and you were drinking a huge amount of water. I watched you drink and was amazed once again by how nice it was to look at you, all warm and velvety, swallowing this mellifluous water. I placed my tilted head in my palm. When I was sufficiently drunk I asked you hey so why are you scared.

You thought about it, and said, well you are complicated.

Okay, and?

And I'm flat, you said, as you drank some more (flat) water.

Nobody is flat, I said.

No, I am, and you will find that out sooner or later.

Oh, come on, I said. I laughed. My entire soul was laughing as I thought how cute it is to say such a thing at a place where everyone else is busy flaunting their personality. But you looked sincere, so sincere that you began to make honorable efforts to peel your colors off, one by one, until you really became a colorless form sitting there drinking water and poking at your gnocchi with a fork. You were doing it so violently that by the end of it you looked like a lost item. By the end of it I could no longer see you. You were nowhere to be seen. I thought about a special camera I once read about somewhere. A camera imitating the human eye. You see, the way we perceive is very efficient, we perceive changes. Neurons in the eye fire only when they sense a change, so that whatever is unchanging, stable, will not be taken in. And this video camera works just that way. It only captures movement. And right now you are staying very very still and you are disappearing in front of my eyes. What? He said. Nothing, I said, (did I really just say all of that out loud?) well, what I meant is that there are certain physical boundaries to what an image can represent. Seeing something is unseeing other things. It's like the unconscious mind must be real, well I'm using the word *real* loosely, the unconscious mind must be real because focusing our attention on anything at all requires unthinkingly repressing our attention to many other things. And when we frame a photo there must be many many things we leave out. How often do we say *you see*? While in fact we don't see. We don't actually. What we don't see is the frame itself. What we don't see is the slaughtering, butchering, quartering, twitching, boiling alive, of each part of an animal, the entrails, tongue, liver, brain, heart. What we don't see is the tedium of the kitchen, the servitude, with no meaning at all ascribed to all that labor, the never-ending labor by those who are often forced to engage in a pleasure that requires submission. We don't see any of that. We are presented, instead, with the essential, the pure, the ultimate artifice. And how possible is it that when we see the beautiful silky flesh on a plate, leaning listlessly in a glistening lake of sauce, we are also on some level aware of the ugly, the cruel, the clumsy attempt to beautify? So we feel guilty, we feel disgusted, we throw up, we purge ourselves clean, we preserve our emptiness by refusing to eat.

He did not say another word and I began to realize how

menacing, really, I was. I looked up. Behind him was a mirror. A gorgeous mirror imitating the gilded age. Mirrors are treacherous things. Sometimes I wondered what I was seeing when I looked into the mirror. Standing in front of the mirror I was often hyper-aware that it was I, I who created this image of me, through looking. Sometimes I felt that the real person I was seeking was hovering somewhere else, pushed aside by the act of looking. And that reality was but the trace left behind by a vanishing, or something being vanished. Sometimes I tried to see my reflection as objectively as I could, as someone else looking from a different angle might see it. I would move my arm a bit and see that it was doing the same thing, but somehow I would detect a slight delay, a hesitation, a perhaps imaginary or purely hypothetical interval where this reflection of mine reflected upon my order and only then decided to follow. And I was suddenly afraid. I was afraid of what this body in the mirror might do and I was afraid that at some point it might no longer be the perfect replica of whatever things I wanted it to do and it would eventually get away from me. Then I would whisper something to that body in the mirror, something cold and cruel. But this time it was all very simple. In the mirror I saw a girl, holding a glass half empty. She had a spiteful face.

I pitied him for having to see that, so I stopped thinking.

Then I said, but I like the way you see things.

He lifted his eyes. Flattered, he said.

He was looking down at that gnocchi mash on his plate, looking like it had been digested already. A strand of his hair fell and covered part of his forehead, and even that seemed to be staged. He was considering something.

After a while he looked at me and asked, can we go now?

Sure, I said.

We got the check. I insisted on paying. Well I drank a lot, I said. But in fact it was because of how old I felt at the moment, but I couldn't tell him that.

When we walked out of the restaurant I lit a cigarette. The night was just descending. We were walking straight into it, into a night like dark waves laden with things unlikely and desirable. Walking, I said to him, let's not do this again.

Okay, he said. Then he looked down at my legs and said, Jesus, you are bleeding.

Yeah, I said.

When I told Frankie that he was scared of me she said, of course, what do you expect. Frankie was looking into the mirror trying to make her brows symmetrical. Do they look symmetrical to you she asked. Yes I said. Are you sure she asked. Yes they are I said. I gazed at the vase on her shelf in the shape of female thighs and her t-shirt with boobs printed on the chest. I thought about the two-ness again. I didn't know how I felt about this type of merchandise ostensibly celebrating feminine beauty, just like I didn't know how I felt about a papaya. Frankie looked back into the mirror, still studying her brows, unconvinced. I sat on the floor, hugging my knees and putting my chin on top of them. I asked her, do you think by calling food porn *food porn* we are doing something crazy here, we are actually saying no to everything the phallus has to offer? Frankie turned around and scanned me from head to toe. No, she said, I love food and I love dicks. Gotcha I said.

We were going to a party. Tuesday nights were for Franklin Street. Before we set out Frankie looked at my feet imploringly and handed me a pair of her shoes. I can't remember what they looked like, just that they were black and they hurt tremendously. We were walking on knives. Frankie was shouting, I'm never wearing heels again. She was always saying that.

I was bleeding so much these days that I had to stick together three sanitary pads like some collage art until they turned into what felt like a giant diaper. Every hour the pads were completely drenched and my loins were heavy with big blood bags. My blood wouldn't go away. I thought about a moist essay by Lao She we read in middle school, about this famous spring. In fact they were three famous springs side by side, always rolling, day and night, all year round. Always lively, always vivid. They never tire, never back down. You really should start using tampons Frankie said. She knew I never liked tampons. Is it anti-feminist to not like tampons? I said it's just uncomfortable. You are not doing it right she said. What I couldn't tell her was that I was afraid of *not* seeing the blood. I need to see, to smell, to understand.

I followed Frankie to her car. I always waited for her to get in the driver's seat before getting in as well. I always waited for her to shut her door first before shutting mine as well. You are too polite Frankie said. It's not like that I thought. It's more like I feel I need permission. Frankie began to play a song in her car. There was a certain theme to the songs Frankie liked to play that year. Young, Dumb & Broke. Stressed Out. Waste A Moment. I leaned against the window as Frankie drove and nodded to the beats. She wanted to know what was going on with me and my boys. I'm beginning to think it's not really about the boys, I said. I thought excess is subversive, and then I thought emptiness is subversive, but in the end we still have to fill ourselves up with something. Even emptiness has a meaning and it's too much to bear. Frankie said, uh oh. Precisely I said.

I forgot to mention that my chest still hurt. It made so little sense that sometimes I even forgot about it.

The last party, Frankie announced, as we got out of her car. But seriously, why are we always going to these parties, I asked. When we were walking through the door of the club I thought about what my advisor had said, college changes people no doubt. A college experience that includes the delirious joys and sharp, sometimes maddening pains of wanting to understand one another, of wanting to touch another being—in your case, through writing I'm sure—is transformative in a more profound way. How hyperbolic does that sound? My advisor enjoys sending people bowls of chicken soup, I thought, and this time it even comes with a giant spoon. Then I thought about a text message I read, saying that we are all scavengers for meager nutrition in the trash. I shook my head to get these words out. No, not tonight. Frankie and I were walking through the door of the club and were soon surrounded by others. We put our heads against each other's like we were little birds. Then Frankie was heading towards the bar, and I watched her walk away fearing that this might be the last image I had of her. I didn't know why I'd think that. Tequila shots for everyone! Last party! We are graduating and now is the last chance to hook up with that someone you've always wanted to hook up with, or to dance on the table or get into the cage or ride the mechanical bull or be fetishized by someone in some way for one night while doing all of the above. Tequila shots made me sick, especially on an empty stomach, but I was downing another one. I'd probably have to throw up very soon but for the moment everything was good. Frankie was taking a selfie with a friend which would soon become an Instagram story or a Snap. But there was no food in sight. Nothing for us to stare at with hunger, to stimulate our appetite, to increase our cravings, and then, most crucially, to renounce it all in a tortuous battle of wills as if we have, once again, tested our power over our desires and practiced starvation as a mode of expression. The two-ness of a woman's desire sets in motion the movement of exhibition and of chaste retreat in order to stimulate the drives of the subject, which is to say, there is a much deeper meaning to *playing hard to get.* Perhaps we are not playing. Perhaps we simply are. Hard to get. And I'm using that terrifying *we* again.

At some point I walked up the stairs to the terrace. Smoke was blurring everyone's eyes. Smoke was pale and light. I squatted next to some precarious banisters and began to type a note:

> the problematic relationship we have with food is, at times, a translation from our even more profound problems with sex itself.
>
> #Foodporn emblematizes the fundamental conflict that women face: you must starve, but you must desire; you have to be chaste, but you have to, at the same time, be sexually desirable.
>
> "I'm starting to think that the phrase 'absence makes the heart grow fonder' was in fact coined by an anorexic."
>
> the ambivalent desire that individuals express towards anorexia is arguably not for thinness as an end goal, but for the absence itself.
>
> Thus #foodporn resolves the paradox for the anorexic,
>
> in a similar way the bulimic swallows and throws up— the paradox of treating food as the object of desire, and ascertaining the emptiness by refusing to eat.

I got the idea of this project at a most strange time in my life. During the many months living with an eating disorder and continuous unnameable pain, I caught myself browsing food images more frequently, subscribing to certain #foodporn accounts, and indulging in a sort of unsituated pleasure.

Later on, I realized that I was not the only one in this reverie: I discovered many fellow "#foodporn addicts," a name we (ab) used jokingly, who were also having a "troubling" relationship with food. Considering the sacrifice—her rejection of her proper pleasure and her embrace of the ideas and ideals of the patriarchal society, inextricably bound with the notion of capital itself—a woman must make to enter the realms previously dominated by men, this new form of pornography is merely the aftermath; it is reactionary.

I allowed myself to sit on the floor, instead of squatting. My legs were numb from squatting too long. So was my left chest. I looked around. I knew some of the faces around me, but it was the faces I didn't know that were looking back at me. It's been a pleasure to have never met you, I thought. I gave that greeting sincerely to each one of them. And one day, I thought, one glorious day, I would begin to remember our very first conversation. I didn't like to think about it very much. I probably never did, until that one day. I would be doing other things, like folding a shirt, eating an apple, or just looking at someone else, and suddenly the words would come back to me, along with the memory of gazing at my phone raised over my face for ten hours straight. During that long conversation the room must have gone from light to dark to light again and my roommate must have started and stopped snoring. Many things must have changed. But I always believed it all happens today, is happening, like a pain without history. Until one day. One day I would suddenly remember everything. Perhaps with amusement. Perhaps with regret. But whatever emotions I house within me is not important. What's important is that I would be *remembering* it. I would finally notice the change of light. The passage of time. Then it would become yesterday, three days ago, and then, weeks and months and years ago.

I didn't know how long I had been sitting like that when the guy began to talk to me. The moment he got my attention I still hadn't recognized him as the German guy from my nine o' clock seminar. We were staring at the railings that divided the party and the fall. He gave me a cigarette. It was then I recognized him, but to this day I still wasn't sure it really was that German guy from the nine o' clock seminar. When he found me I was not ready to be found. We sat there like two people who forgot their mother tongues. We actually were two people who forgot their mother tongues. Neither of us seemed to have the strength to carry on a conversation of any sort when we were surrounded by licensed absurdities of others. I realized we hadn't spoken a word since he passed me that cigarette. Where have we left off? *Life and Fate*, right? Is it too late to get back to that? But I really don't want to get back to that. The German guy was then slowly rubbing his temples. I was about to make an excuse to leave when, for some reason, he began to talk about mushrooms. Mushrooms in Luxembourg. It took me a few minutes to understand he was really talking about actual mushrooms. He would drive across the border to pick mushrooms in forests. Sometimes he was fazed by strange-looking ones but he still couldn't help picking them because you see they were so strange, almost like a mistake and because of that, almost beautiful. He sent the pictures of the ones that looked like mistakes to his grandmother. His grandmother would tell him, yes, this, we used to eat a lot when we were little. So he would feel encouraged to eat them too. While he was still wandering in the forest picking mushrooms he would think about what he could do with them. Yes, he could slice the mushrooms and grill them with butter.

Or he could make mushroom sauce which would have a splendid scent that reminds us of where they came from, where we came from. So one day, as usual, he was following a path in the forest, picking mushrooms from the wet soil, when he stepped into shit. Human shit, and a sizable dump at that. How do you know it's human shit I asked. It could very well be dogshit I said. Because next to the shit there was some toilet paper he said. Unbelievable, he said, the shitter actually brought with them some toilet paper when they headed into the forest. Thorough, I said. For some reason I couldn't get the image out of my head. Shit in the forest. Mushrooms growing out of shit. We are all scavengers. Quite literally. The German guy finished his cigarette. I turned around and the party-goers were all doing various extravagant things with their bodies believing that they looked very good when they did that. The German guy looked as well. I wasn't sure if we were seeing the same thing.

I printed out notes on my phone, and put them side by side with notes on various pieces of paper, papers of all imaginable colors and shapes: the back of a menu, a leaflet from the conference, a receipt I got from the hospital, napkins, chopstick sleeves, paper coasters with the name of the bar. In the end I had managed to create a huge mess.

There was music downstairs in the quad and the impatient air of spring was getting through the open window. I continued to type. While I typed and typed and typed I had a strange feeling of intoxication enabled by the youth of others. I worked like that for several days, going to sleep only when I couldn't keep my eyes open, eating only when I absolutely had to, while the music downstairs kept growing louder and louder day by day, there was no end to it, they didn't want anything to end, it seemed, and somehow that backdrop seemed to imply to me that my endeavors here would never end. Then I felt that when I finally stopped writing all music would stop too and the whole world would be gone and I would die, we would all die. I couldn't imagine how I could continue to be once this thing was finished, how I would rise again from my desk and shake off all the ashes and debris and stand face to face with life again.

(Today, when I have a long nap in the afternoon and wake up to a hit song from that year outside my window my first thought is, I have to get back to my thesis. My mind manages to construct a mysterious connection between spring, music from that year, and writing, and during those few seconds of waking up, many years later, when the connection is immediately, effortlessly made I need no convincing to feel I'm that twenty-two year old again, with all my colors still intact, with all my pain still loud and clear—which in retrospect might seem insignificant and melodramatic—to whom the end of everything seems alarmingly near, an end which, to the person many years later, would just be another memory.)

I would fall asleep and wake up because of the pain. I would fall asleep despite the pain. Medicine replaced the hours. Cigarettes replaced the minutes. You replaced the days and years. But who are you? I woke up with a bitter taste in my mouth like memories from a darker hemisphere. My blood still wouldn't stop flowing. I knocked on the walls of my theoretical maze and waited in vain for echoes. I told you, yeah so I guess I just need some echoes. Go to a studio or something you said. But who are you?

For a while I didn't move. I couldn't move. Then I got more comfortable. Once I got comfortable with the idea—the idea that there was no truth in what I was doing nor was there any way to redeem it—everything seemed easier. I lay on the carpeted floor and bit into a piece of paper. I began to chew something. A while later I sat up and began to leaf through *The Aesthetics of Resistance* by Peter Weiss, one of the books assigned by the professor from the nine o' clock seminar:

> *It would again and again seem as though all earlier hopes would be brought to nothing by lost or forgotten intentions. And even if it did not turn out as we hoped, nothing would be changed about those hopes themselves. Hoping should be necessary.*

Hoping is necessary, I thought, and Sisyphus (yes, him again) should be happy. It was then I knew I finally had my ending. I sat up straight and started to write:

Il faut imaginer Sisyphe heureux. My project starts with, and is sustained by, this necessary imagination.

I wrote:

Even though, the dream that #foodporn promises, like every other fantasy in the history of desire, is doomed to be unsatisfying, it is precisely this failure that enables desire. We are never truly loyal to successes, but we are always loyal to lost causes.

I had to stop there, because at that moment I got a phone call from you. It's me you said. Of course I said, it has always been you. Hearing your voice was like hearing my own end. I shifted to the window. Everything goes in full circle. You told me that you were in Los Angeles, at some hobnobbing event, and you were trying to sell your film to wives of coal bosses, the same people who messed up the hearts and lungs of others so that Frankie had a thesis to write. Okay I said, it's fine, what can we do. You sounded tired but you didn't sigh, thank god. You see we have been feeding each other pictures of ourselves because we have nothing to say and even less to offer. Time and time again we try to rewrite a script that was already finalized. We watch the sun seeping through unfamiliar blinds like mud. And I could no longer tell which is true and which is self-deception, the creation of a situation. You laughed. You said I talked different now. You said I was ruined now. You sent over a video. During your down time you watched the busy bees in a natural history museum, and the people around you gathered and dispersed. I told you this moment was a lot like your film, frame by frame, frozen. You saw the film? God I'm so ashamed of it you said. Then there were masses of silence. You were perhaps spreading yourself out on a different floor. At the border between spring and summer, the heating in your room was still on, free of charge. Fine beads of sweat seeped out from your pores. Unhurriedly. And I could no longer tell which was true and which was fiction. I told you about my recent discovery, that it is no longer possible to imagine a true utopian sociality where vulnerability is not retaliated with betrayal, or with disillusionment. Therefore suffering in others is absurd, sympathy is horrific, and sincerity, grotesque. Therefore we have to work, we have to eat. Day and night. We have to love again and again to convince ourselves that it is impossible. Therefore I don't blame you. Smart people watch soap operas too, you said, we cannot always lie on the ground. What are you doing? I asked. Opening a window, you said.

Acknowledgments

To all my beautiful friends, especially F., Y., and B. (for your words, your brilliance, your complicity, your kindness), to Josh and Story and Catherine and everyone at Game Over Books (for making it happen), and to L., thank you.

Biography

Sienna Liu is a writer and literary translator living in New York City. She is the author of *Specimen* (Split/Lip Press, forthcoming in 2025) and *Square* (Black Sunflowers Poetry Press, 2022). Her English-to-Chinese translations include Rachel Cusk's *Second Place* (Guangxi Normal University Press, 2023), Claire-Louise Bennett's *Checkout 19* (forthcoming), Ali Smith's *Companion Piece* (forthcoming), and a new translation of Virginia Woolf's *Mrs. Dalloway* (forthcoming).